Duffy's rough chin was rubbing the skin on her own as his mouth moved back and forth against her lips, his wet tongue moistening them from time to time. Caroline parted her lips to let his tongue gain access to her mouth, and it immediately thrust inside, filling her mouth with its driving force.

Caroline began imperceptibly to move her breasts back and forth against his chest, inflaming herself to the point where she knew she'd have trouble standing if he were to let go of her. She felt weak all over, weak and yet sexually alive in every nerve of her body. Caroline wanted Duffy's naked body against her own, to arrive at that place where she could no longer think, no longer make decisions. She broke off the kiss, staring intently into his surprised eyes. "Make love to me, Duffy...."

Dear Reader,

It is our pleasure to bring you romance novels that go beyond category writing. The settings of **Harlequin American Romance** give a sense of place and culture that is uniquely American, and the characters are warm and believable. The stories are of "today" and have been chosen to give variety within the vast scope of romance fiction.

This romance is as American as one can get. America's "finest" are represented here: the golden arches, wines from the vineyards of California, a singing chicken expressing the love of the hero, and a New York Jet. If you enjoyed *City Life, City Love,* you will adore Beverly Sommers's latest effort.

From the early days of Harlequin, our primary concern has been to bring you novels of the highest quality. **Harlequin American Romance** is no exception. Enjoy!

Vivian Stephens

Vivian Stephens
Editorial Director
Harlequin American Romance
919 Third Avenue,
New York, N.Y. 10022

Unscheduled Love

BEVERLY SOMMERS

Harlequin Books

TORONTO • NEW YORK • LONDON
AMSTERDAM • PARIS • SYDNEY • HAMBURG
STOCKHOLM • ATHENS • TOKYO • MILAN

Published October 1983

First printing August 1983

ISBN 0-373-16026-7

Printed in Canada

Chapter One

Caroline's first clue was the sight of her black silk teddy dangling from the brass bedpost of her queen-sized bed. Then her eyes traveled downward to the array of underclothes strewn across the carpeted floor. There was no mistake about it. She might be somewhat messy, but *that* messy she wasn't.

She retraced her steps into the living room and saw at once that one of the windows to the fire escape was open. She looked around, but nothing seemed to have been touched. She closed the window. It was futile at this point, but if nothing else, it was letting in hot, humid air. She switched on the air conditioner and, deciding she'd probably never make it to the gym that night, went to the refrigerator and got herself a cold bottle of beer.

Psychologically she had been prepared for it. She had heard about the crime in New York, been warned to keep a tight grasp on her purse at all times, and had even taken a course in self-defense in order to be able to walk the streets at night. She hadn't given much thought to burglary, because the building was in a good neighborhood and had seemed secure. Well, so much for security!

She found her Manhattan telephone directory and looked up the emergency number for the police. She dialed the number, was connected to a police precinct, and immediately put on hold. That upset her most of all. She was proud of her ability to remain unruffled in emergencies, but to be put on *hold*? What if the burglar were still on the premises? What if she were being attacked? What good was an emergency number if the end result was that she was put on hold?

She took a long drink of the beer and lit a cigarette. She had smoked it halfway down before an officer came on the line, not even apologizing for the delay. She explained that someone had broken into her apartment and was asked what was stolen. Caroline glanced around. The color TV was still in its place, as was the Betamax. The stereo hadn't been touched. The furniture, what there was of it, was all in place.

She told the officer she hadn't looked thoroughly enough to make sure what was taken and what wasn't, it seeming inconceivable to her that perhaps nothing had been taken.

He told her to look around carefully and make a list of anything that was missing and that a detective would be at her place within an hour.

The living room didn't appear to have anything

missing. She went into the bedroom, viewing the mess with distaste, and looked in the top dresser drawer where she kept the small amount of jewelry she owned. The drawers had been messed up a bit, but her jewelry was all there. It looked as though all her underwear was there, too. Not neatly folded, of course, but artfully displayed about the room. She hated to think what kind of nut could have done that.

She was in no mood to start itemizing her underwear. Instead she grabbed the key to her apartment and decided to pay a visit to the superintendent of the building.

She hadn't seen the woman since the month before when she had signed the lease to the apartment. Even though Caroline didn't have any friends in the city and the woman wasn't much older than herself, she was the kind of garrulous character Caroline usually tried to avoid. When Chloe McMahon had asked her questions about where she worked and how much salary she earned, she hadn't demurred. Those were the kind of questions a rental agent had a right to ask, she felt, but when she had been asked her astrological sign, she had refused to answer. Not only did she believe astrology to be pure nonsense, but she was afraid her sign would turn out to be one not in Chloe's favor or perhaps one that signified some weakness that would render her an unsuitable tenant. And she had very much wanted the apartment. Since then Caroline had figured things out by herself, such as when to put the trash out, the location of the laundry room, etc., in order to avoid contact with the super.

She knocked on the door of the first floor rear apartment. The door opened and Mahler's Sixth Symphony filled the hallway. Chloe, reading glasses perched on her nose, her orange hair looking as though she had recently been electrocuted, peered out.

"Ms. Hart," she murmured, waving Caroline inside, "come in, come in. Would you like a cup of tea?"

Caroline stepped inside, avoiding two cats that had followed their mistress to the door. "No thanks. I just wanted to tell you that my apartment was burglarized."

"Come in the kitchen, what you need is a hot cup of tea," said Chloe, apparently unperturbed by the news of crime in her building.

Caroline remembered well the herbal variety she had been served when she signed her lease, and again declined. She followed Chloe into the kitchen and took a seat on the one chair not occupied by a cat. The chair was placed in front of an electric typewriter, still turned on, and she averted her eyes from the paper. Unlike Chloe, she was not by nature inquisitive.

"I was just writing my column," Chloe explained, ignoring the fact that Caroline had not wanted tea and setting a cup in front of her. The tea looked green and Caroline was damned if she was going to drink it.

"A column?" she asked.

"I write a monthly astrological column for *Womanspace*," she said, naming a magazine of feminist bent that Caroline had noticed on the newsstands.

Chloe moved a cat and sat down across from her, studying her over the tops of her glasses. "A burglary. Umm. It's too bad I didn't do a chart for you, you would have been warned."

This woman might not be putting her on hold like the police, but it didn't appear she was going to be any more helpful.

"I believe he came in through the window, off the fire escape."

Chloe nodded, obviously waiting for more.

"The strange thing is, I don't think he took anything. I have a TV and a stereo and...well, everything appears to be there."

"Probably looking for drugs," said Chloe.

"In my *underwear*?"

Chloe's eyes widened. "He disturbed your underwear?"

Caroline explained the state in which she had found her underthings while Chloe listened avidly.

"I think we're dealing with a nut here," said Chloe when she had finished. "Have you notified the police?"

Caroline nodded. "I called them right away."

"Not that they'll do anything. They're only interested in big crimes; burglaries happen all the time. Now if you had been attacked, maybe they'd do something.'' Chloe looked over at Caroline's untouched cup. ''Drink your tea!''

''Thank you, no, I really don't care for tea.''

''Drink it anyway—I want to read your tea leaves.''

A super, a writer, and now a fortune-teller? Caroline was beginning to wish she'd just stayed in her apartment and waited for the police. ''I really don't think—'' she began.

Chloe shrugged expressively. ''Listen, it's not a science like astrology, but sometimes I sense things.''

''What I sense,'' said Caroline firmly, ''is that I need some protection over my windows. Whoever that nut is, I don't want him returning.''

''Call the locksmith across the street,'' advised Chloe.

''I thought maybe the landlord...''

''No way! Other tenants have tried and he won't pay for them.'' She got up from the table and went over to a bulletin board, removing a card and handing it to Caroline. ''Tell Duffy I sent you and he'll give you a good price.''

Caroline put the card in her jacket pocket and stood up.

''Aren't you going to drink your tea?''

''I have to go upstairs and wait for the police. But thank you, I'll let you know what happens.''

''I wish you'd tell me your sign and let me make

a chart for you. I like to know about the people who are living in the building."

"You've made charts for everyone?"

Chloe nodded. "Everyone but you. No charge, of course. What I need is your date and time of birth and where you were born."

Not wanting to get into an argument about astrology, Caroline wrote down the information for her, then took the offered copy of *Womanspace* that Chloe thrust at her, telling Caroline she got the copies free from the publishers.

When the police arrived ten minutes later, Caroline was reading Chloe's column and laughing out loud. She had occasionally glanced at her horoscope before in magazines or newspapers, but always found them to be nonsense. Chloe's was nonsense too, but written in such an ironically witty way that she found herself reading every one. She wrote such things as,

The fifteenth should be a perfect day to start a new romance and while a tall dark stranger would be perfect, with your luck it will probably turn out to be a bill collector. My advice is not to open the door to any strange men, tall and dark included.

When the doorbell rang Caroline looked through the peephole and saw two men. Deciding it wasn't likely that the burglar had come back with a friend and was using the door this time, she opened it and gave a cursory glance at the men's ID before letting them inside.

They didn't do any of the things she expected the police to do. They didn't dust for fingerprints or look out on the fire escape for footprints or any other kind of clues. They looked around, a little longer at her underwear than she felt was warranted, and then asked her if she had made up a list of what was taken.

"The most we can do is notify the pawnshops in case anything turns up," one of them said, then looked relieved when she told them nothing was stolen.

The other one suggested she get herself a dog. "Burglars don't like to mess around with large, vicious dogs," he said rather laconically.

"Neither do I," said Caroline, preferring the unknown burglar to the known dog who might turn on her at any time. To say nothing of having to walk him several times a day!

"I suggest you get a locksmith over here," said the other one as they prepared to leave. "This neighborhood gets a lot of burglaries. Nice apartments, you know?"

She hadn't known, but wasn't about to live in a slum area just to avoid burglars. She opened the door for them, then locked it after they left, as per their instructions. However, she didn't know what good it did to lock the door, when the burglar came in through the window.

She took the card Chloe had given her out of her

pocket. "Murray Hill Security," it read, gave the owner's name as Stephen Duffy and a telephone number to call. She remembered receiving fliers from the shop when she had first moved in. Many fliers, in fact, all of which she had immediately thrown out wondering at the time how she had gotten on a list for junk mail so quickly. Curious if the store would still be open, she walked over to the window and looked down. The garish green sign was still lit and she thought she could see lights on in the shop.

She called the number on the card and the phone was answered by a deep, pleasant voice. She explained that her apartment had been broken into and that the police had suggested she call a locksmith. He told her he didn't have time that night, but could stop by first thing in the morning.

"If I wait until morning I'll probably change my mind," said Caroline, wondering why no one seemed to take a burglary at all seriously.

"Well," said the voice at the other end, seemingly hesitating.

"I'm right across the street from you, it wouldn't take long," she said hopefully.

"You're at one-forty-two?"

"Yes. Apartment Four A."

There was a short pause, then, "All right, I'll come over right now."

She hung up with a sigh of relief. Maybe a simple burglar alarm at the window would do the trick. She looked at her watch that gave the date and time and other information in such minute detail she almost needed a magnifying glass to read it, and decided she would definitely not have time to visit the gym. Tomorrow was Saturday, though; she'd make it up then.

She was heading for the kitchen for a second beer, the first one having gone warm and flat, when her doorbell rang. She took a quick look through the peephole, then opened the door wide to let the locksmith in.

She was appraising his tall, slim build, black curly hair and deep blue eyes when she caught the fleeting looks of surprise and then anger cross his face. Although why he should be angry, she couldn't figure out.

"Just like that you open the door?" he said, walking past her into the apartment. "Weren't you just robbed or have I got the wrong apartment?"

Caroline felt instant annoyance at the tone of his voice. What she didn't need was some lecture from a locksmith, probably in an effort to sell her something she didn't need. "I think twice in one day would be a bit of a coincidence," she told him, watching the way his blue eyes seemed to darken.

His eyes glanced quickly around the living room, then settled on her. "Is that what you think? Well, you're wrong. There are some people who are born victims, did you know that? I saw some guy on the Channel Four News—he's been mugged over three hundred times, a couple of times twice in one day."

Caroline kept her expression bland. "I'm not a born victim."

He leaned against the wall, his hands in his pockets. "You're not going to ask me who I am? Ask for some ID?"

"I called Murray Hill Security, your shirt says Murray Hill Security, ergo..."

"You didn't know that before you opened the door."

"In addition to being a born victim, I'm also psychic," she said, sarcasm oozing to the surface of her speech.

"If you were really psychic, you'd have called me yesterday," he said, obviously bent on having the last word. "Lesson number one: Keep your door locked!"

"I do keep my door locked."

"They why is it open now?"

Caroline sighed in exasperation. "Because I thought you might like to take a look at it, see if the lock is adequate. That's what you're here for, isn't it?"

He glanced over at the front door. "I could tell that lock wasn't adequate the minute I saw it. Anyone could open it with a credit card."

"Terrific," mumbled Caroline.

"Right—now lock it!"

Caroline went over to the door, slammed it, then turned the lock. "Satisfied?"

"You're learning."

She faced him, her arms folded in front of her.

"Just tell me the point of locking it if anyone can open it with a credit card?"

"Just trying to teach you good habits."

Caroline turned to go into the living room. "The man on the phone was a lot more pleasant than you."

He chuckled. "That was *me* on the phone. I've been told I have a charming telephone manner."

"Too bad it doesn't extend to personal confrontations."

His eyes narrowed as he studied her for a moment, then he straightened up, headed for the door, unlocked it, opened it, stepped outside and slammed it behind him.

Caroline just stood there, wondering why he had gotten so temperamental all of a sudden, when there was a knock on the door. She opened it and he stood there smiling politely, a smile that didn't fool her for one moment.

"Good evening, miss. I'm from Murray Hill Security, are you Miss Hart?"

"Very funny," she muttered, making a big production out of locking the door behind him after he stepped inside.

He was still looking down at her with a smile. "How did you hear about Murray Hill Security, anyway, if I may ask?"

"Are you kidding? I must have gotten a million of your fliers since I moved in. Anyway, you're right across the street. Every time I look out of the window I see your sign."

"Yeah, that's a nice sign—draws a lot of attention. Have the police been here yet?"

"They left a little while ago."

She followed him into the living room and watched as he opened one of the windows and stuck his head out.

"He must have got in through here," he remarked.

Brilliant deduction, she thought. "Yes, I guess he didn't have a credit card."

He stood back and looked at the windows. "Why don't you have these covered?"

"I haven't gotten around to it yet."

"You shouldn't leave them like this, anyone can just look in."

She could sense another lecture in the offing and she briefly wondered why attractive men always seemed to turn out to be the most annoying. "So what?"

He raised one black brow. "You want people looking in at you?"

"What difference does it make? It's only the living room."

"They can see you in here, can't they?"

"See me *what*? Working? What's the big deal?" She sat down at the table and lit a cigarette, wishing she had never called him.

"That's all you do in here? Work?"

He and Chloe would get along fine; they both shared a proclivity for being nosy. "Occasionally I eat."

He was sitting on the windowsill now, leaning back against the window. "You don't mind people watching you?"

"Oh, for heaven's sake—I don't mind them watching me in restaurants!"

"That's different. You ought to have more privacy in your own home."

She would prefer more privacy at the moment. "Oh, come on—how many people are going to be fascinated by watching me eat? Or work?"

"You'd be surprised," he said, slipping once more into his lecture voice. "There are a lot of people who like to watch other people, see how they live, what they do. They watch you for a while, pretty soon they begin to think they know you. They maybe see you on the street, you look familiar to them... You an exhibitionist or something?"

"Are you crazy?" She felt herself fast losing her temper.

He was looking around the room. "Doesn't look like he took anything big. I see you still got your stereo and TV."

Caroline was wishing she had another beer. But then she'd feel obliged to offer one to him and somehow didn't think that would be a very good idea. He seemed to be making himself too much at home as it was. "He didn't take anything at all," she informed him.

"You kidding me?"

"Well, I'm not too neat, but I don't see anything missing. I looked when the police were here."

"You're not missing *anything*?"

"I don't think so."

He let out a low whistle. "I'd call that lucky."

"I'd call it creepy."

"You'd rather be robbed? That's crazy."

The hell with him. She was going to have a beer whether he was there or not. She took one out of the refrigerator and opened it, watching him over the top of the breakfast bar, then her natural courtesy took over and she held it out to him. He shook his head, and she took a long swallow before answering him. "I don't think it's crazy. What kind of person would break in here just to look through my things, find out about me? A weirdo, right?"

He shrugged. "Sounds like it might have been someone you know."

"That's what the police said. But I don't know anyone that well. Not in New York, anyway."

His eyes seemed to darken again. "A jealous boyfriend maybe?"

"No. None of the men I know would do something like that." Actually, she couldn't think of any man that interested in her.

"Maybe you don't know them as well as you think."

"You've got to be involved to get jealous. I don't get involved."

"Never?"

"Never."

"How do you manage that?" he asked, interest in his voice.

She lit another cigarette and looked at him in annoyance. "Isn't this conversation getting a little personal?"

He laughed and shrugged.

"I liked you better on the phone," she said, hoping to get on with the business at hand.

"You'd rather speak to a recording than the real thing?"

"That wasn't a recording."

"How do you know?"

"Because you asked questions."

He stood up. "Just testing your alertness. Are these the only windows in the place?"

She shook her head. "There's one in the bedroom."

"Mind if I take a look?"

"That's what you're here for," she said sarcastically, pointing out the bedroom door to him. He disappeared from her sight before she remembered she hadn't picked up her underwear. Oh well, it would obviously be the cause of another lecture, but she'd try to keep her temper in check this time. No sense in letting him see he annoyed her.

He had a big grin on his face when he came back in. "I think you were right—the guy *is* a weirdo, unless *you* hang your underwear from the bedposts."

"No, I do not!"

"Just wondering. Anyway, the window in the bedroom is safe enough, just opens on an air shaft. Is there a window in the bathroom?"

"A tiny one, but it's painted shut."

He took a measuring tape out of his pocket and started to measure the living room windows.

"You don't have to measure them to see they're big enough for a man to get through," she said.

"You one of those liberated women?"

"Why?"

"Just wondering why you're assuming it was a man."

"I *know* it was a man. Women aren't weirdos."

"You should meet some of the ones *I* meet in this business, you wouldn't say that."

"You really think some woman hung my underwear from the bedposts?"

He looked at her, a slow smile spreading across his face. "You think that's not possible?" His eyes slowly traveled down the length of her body. "Hell, I mean look at you—a suit, a tie..."

Caroline felt herself flush. "What exactly are you inferring, Mr. Duffy?"

He assumed a look of innocence. "Not a thing." He paused, and then, "Do you always dress like a man?"

Caroline thought she looked good in her khaki cotton suit, white silk shirt blouse and narrow red tie. "Any other personal questions you'd like to get out of the way?"

He sat down at the table beside her and took out a pad and pencil from his pocket. He did some quick figuring, then looked over at her with a smile. "I apologize for that last remark. You are femininity personified!"

Sensing he was being just as sarcastic as she had been previously, she ignored the remark.

"Now, for the estimate. The front door's simple. I can fix you up with a lock that nobody can pick— put it on for you for fifty bucks. Usually I charge sixty-five, but I'm making this a package deal. For the windows you're going to need windowgates."

"What?"

"Windowgates. You've probably seen them on stores—"

"I know what they are. But I don't want any."

He leaned back in his chair. "I'm sure you're aware your windows lead out to a fire escape."

"Of course I'm aware—I sunbathe out there."

"Ah—that explains it!"

"Explains *what*?"

"The fetishist."

She shook her head in disbelief. "The what?"

"A fetishist is someone—"

"I know what a fetishist is," she almost shouted.

"Do you wear a bikini when you sunbathe?"

"What if I do?"

"So, you sit out on that fire escape, half naked, for anyone to see."

"What's the difference whether I sit out there or on the beach?" She had never met such an exasperating man in her entire life.

"Obviously someone living in that building across the street is an underwear fetishist. He—or she— saw you out on the fire escape in what appeared to be underwear, then broke in today to get a closer look. Which explains the scene in the bedroom." He sounded very satisfied with himself.

"You're a nut, do you know that?"

"But not a fetishist."

"I only have your word for that," said Caroline, getting up and moving away from him. He was laughing now, but she wasn't amused. "Anyway, no windowgates. How would I get out in case of a fire?"

"Personally, I'd use the stairs. But they do open from the inside. You can get out but no one can get in."

Caroline lit another cigarette and sat on the arm of the couch. "I don't feel like living in a cage."

He chuckled. "It would stifle your free spirit, right? Am I right?" he repeated when she didn't answer.

"I like a sense of freedom," Caroline admitted.

"Well, I'm afraid you're going to have to choose between a sense of freedom and a sense of security."

She thought of seeing bars every time she looked out the window. "I don't like feeling closed in."

He chuckled. "Oh, one of those claustrophobics, huh?"

She shot him an angry look. "Despite what you think, I'm not an exhibitionist, or a claustrophobic, Mr. Duffy."

"You can just call me Duffy, all my friends do."

"I don't want to call you Duffy!"

"How about Stephen?"

"Listen, Mr. Duffy—"

"Drink your beer, calm down, relax. I know you've been through a traumatic experience today."

He was the only thing that seemed to be traumatizing her at the moment. "What are you, the neighborhood shrink?"

"I did major in psychology," he admitted.

"Just what I needed—an intellectual locksmith!"

"I'll tell you something, Miss—do you have a first name?"

"Yes, I do."

"Am I allowed to know it?"

"It's Caroline, but you can call me Ms. Hart."

"Well, Ms. Caroline Hart, I don't consider myself a high-pressure salesman, but in your case I'd strongly suggest you have some windowgates put on those windows." He handed her a slip of paper with figures scrawled on it. "Here's what I'll charge you. Call in another place for a second estimate if you like. But please—don't take the chance of this happening again. You might be asleep in the bedroom next time. And *he* might want more than just to hang up your underwear, if you get my meaning."

"Yes, I get your meaning," Caroline said between clenched teeth.

"I thought you would."

She took a good look at the estimate. "That much? To put bars on my windows?"

"Not bars—wrought-iron grillwork. Some people put it up just for decoration. If you can't pay for it all at once..."

"I can afford it," she snapped.

"I figured you could—nice apartment like this and all."

"Do you charge according to how nice the apartment is?"

He appeared to be affronted at the mere suggestion. "Do I look unethical?"

"Yes."

"Thanks a lot." He looked around, appraising the furnishings. "What do you do for a living?"

Caroline stood up and walked to the window. It was later than she thought, the sun was already beginning to set. "More personal questions?" she asked, turning on one of the lamps.

"It seemed harmless enough." He was leaning against the couch now and she wondered if he had a problem standing up.

"I work for an oil company."

"Pumping gas?" He chuckled.

"I'm in charge of mergers and acquisitions." Let him figure that one out if he could.

"I'm impressed. Sounds like hard work," he said, but he didn't look very impressed to her.

"It is." In a minute she'd say yes to the windowgates just to shut him up. Or maybe no, and that way get rid of him instantly. Although a negative answer would probably precipitate another lecture. He should have stuck with psychology; that way he could lecture people all day.

"I bet you like it though, right?"

"I thrive on it!"

He moved away from the couch and leaned against one wall, surreptitiously looking at the titles of her books while he talked. "I can see it now—going to be a millionaire by the time you're thirty, right?"

"Wrong. I'm going to be a vice-president by the time I'm thirty. I'll be a millionaire by the time I'm forty." And thirty wasn't very far off now, she thought.

"And then?"

Tired of his endless questions, she came to a decision. "Look—I'll take the bars. Can you put them in now?"

"You mean tonight?"

"I mean right now."

He grinned. "How about tomorrow morning?"

"If I can survive tonight without the fetishist returning, I might change my mind about having them put in."

He ran one hand through his curly hair, the kind of hair Caroline had always wished she had instead of the perfectly straight variety she had been blessed with. "Tonight's kind of difficult," he mumbled.

"I'll pay extra."

She saw the corner of his mouth twitch. "Is that a bribe?"

"No, it's not!"

"You used to getting your own way with money?"

"It seems to have a miraculous effect on some people." He moved toward the door and she feared she had at last angered him. "Look, Duffy—"

He turned around and smiled. "Ah—softening me up with my name now."

She walked toward the door. "Forget it! I've lived without bars up to now, I'll take my chances."

He paused for a moment. "I'll have to go back to the shop and pick up the windowgates. How about if I'm back in an hour?"

"An hour? To go across the street and back?"

"I haven't eaten yet."

"Neither have I!"

"What are you fixing?" he asked, looking interested.

She smiled at the thought of her empty cupboards. "I'm not fixing anything."

"You're not going to eat?"

"I don't have any food in the house."

"You don't eat?"

"I usually eat out," she snapped, thinking he could start an argument over the most innocuous subjects.

"You want me to pick up some groceries?"

"No, I don't want you to pick up some groceries.

If you have to eat first, okay—I'll go out later."

He shrugged. "Suit yourself." Well, that time she had been rude to him for no reason; he had only tried to be helpful.

"Listen—thanks for putting them in tonight."

"You're welcome," he said. He was just about to the door when he looked up at the moose head she had hanging on the wall. "That moose head kind of catches your eye, if you know what I mean."

"Yes."

"I mean, it's a bit unusual to see a moose head hanging in a woman's apartment."

"No doubt."

"Probably not many in the whole city." He unlocked the door and opened it.

"Probably not," she agreed.

He turned around. "What are you doing with a moose head?" he wanted to know.

"I'm a moose head fetishist," she said, determined to get the last word.

"Lock the door after me," said Duffy, disappearing down the hall.

Chapter Two

Caroline slammed the door and locked it, wishing just once she could manage to get the last word with Duffy. What a truly annoying man he was. She usually got along very well with men on a businesslike basis, and indeed had earned their respect at work. But Duffy! He just wouldn't take her seriously. Well, what could you expect of a locksmith after all. Obviously he lacked any ambition, any seriousness regarding his life. And it wasn't as though he weren't educated—he must have studied psychology in college.

She went into the bedroom and quickly gathered up her underwear, shoving it into the dresser drawers to sort out later. She took off her suit and blouse and hung them up, then got out of her heels and panty hose and breathed a sigh of relief. It was necessary for her to dress as an executive at work, but at home what she demanded in clothes was pure comfort. She got into jeans and a baseball shirt and had just finished tying her Adidas when the doorbell rang. She quickly ran a comb through her straight, shoulder-length hair and answered the door.

Duffy, a layer of sweat on his face, was standing there weighted down with two very large window-gates. He moved past her and set them against the wall as she shut the door and started to lock it.

"Leave it open, I have to get my toolbox," he said, wiping his face off with the arm of his shirt. His eyes slowly surveyed her body and she saw his now-familiar grin. "You weren't satisfied just dressing like a man—you had to dress like a jock!"

She mimicked his stance, legs apart and thumbs hooked into her front pockets. "You know, Duffy, I can really live without your attempts at humor."

He leaned against the wall. "Who's being funny? I'm serious. I can understand why you don't get involved with men. Who would want to put his arms around a woman who looks like she plays for the Jets?"

"I was going to do some exercises. I usually work out at my gym on Friday nights." Which was a lie, at least the first part of it. These were the clothes she wore at home whether she exercised or not.

"I'm disturbing your schedule?"

"I'll make up for it in the morning."

"What happens in the morning?"

Didn't the man ever tire of asking questions? "I generally run, but tomorrow I'll also go to the gym."

His eyes seemed alight with mischief. "In your green running shorts, right?"

She looked at him in silence.

"Am I right?"

"How did you know that?"

"I've seen you a couple of times when I've been opening up in the morning. You really shouldn't run around the city in that get-up—people will get the wrong idea, if you get my meaning."

She folded her arms across her chest. "No, I don't!"

"Hey, that's a pretty sexy outfit, you know." He was looking at her in a way that was making her increasingly uncomfortable. A locksmith, a man who was there to conduct some business, and he had the effrontery to look at her the way a man looks at a woman. She wished for once she could put him in his place. And that he would stay there.

"Running shorts and a T-shirt? How did I go from looking like a jock to looking sexy?"

"Well, those shorts..."

"There are people running all over the city wearing running shorts," she informed him. "You have some pretty strange ideas."

"I'm just trying to tell you, you've got to be a little careful, that's all. What do you run, a mile?"

"Six miles." And maybe if he got some exercise occasionally perhaps he wouldn't have to lean against something to stay upright.

"You must be in good shape. Of course it's hard

to tell, the way you camouflage your body with all those clothes."

"Must you be offensive?" asked Caroline, ready to throw him out if he persisted.

"I'm just being normal. Hey, have you eaten yet?"

"I told you I'd eat later."

He grinned. "Good. I brought some stuff from the deli. Set the table and I'll be back in a minute. And listen, put on something a little more appealing, okay? I have to sit across the table from you."

He quickly went out the door, once more getting in the last word because she was still standing there speechless, her mouth practically hanging open. More appealing? As though that gray uniform shirt and pants he was wearing was in any way appealing. As though she were even interested in appealing to him! Just when men were finally beginning to treat women as equals, she had to meet someone who was a throwback to the old days. Well, she wasn't going to set the table, and she wasn't going to change her clothes, and if there was cleaning up to do after they ate, she wasn't going to do that, either. He was probably one of those men who thought a woman's place was in the kitchen or the bedroom. And she was going to be damn sure he didn't see her in either!

Too bad he had to be so disarmingly attractive. Those black-Irish looks of his got to her every time, particularly since she came from a place where most men were blondes. She was honest enough to admit to herself that she wouldn't have wasted a moment in argument with him or tolerated any of his personal questions if he had just been ordinary looking. His body looked good too, at least what she could see from the shirt and pants he was wearing. Although how someone as lazy as he appeared to be could stay in such good shape, she didn't know. She worked like crazy running and lifting weights just so she could maintain her slim figure. If she didn't, she hated to think what might happen to her shape.

She wondered briefly what he might be like in bed, then immediately dismissed it as an unproductive and even dangerous thought. Anyway, he probably was the type who never shut up in bed. With his mouth, she'd bet on it!

She took out a cigarette then returned it to the pack. He must be making her nervous. She had already smoked more cigarettes than she usually smoked in an entire evening. Of course it could be all the excitement of the burglary too, only she suddenly realized she had totally forgotten about that. It didn't seem real or even particularly scary. Just a little silly that someone could get so carried away with her underwear, most of which was pretty utilitarian anyway, except the black silk teddy, an impulse buy, which she had never even had occasion to wear.

Duffy walked in, toolbox in one hand and a brown paper grocery sack in the other. He looked at the bare table on the way to the kitchen but didn't say a word. He opened cupboard doors and in a matter of minutes the table was set and an appetizing array of delicatessen food was set out for their immediate consumption.

Caroline had thought of declining his offer of food, but once having seen it she couldn't resist. "Would you like something to drink?" she asked him.

"What have you got?"

"I have some wine."

"What kind?" he said in a supercilious voice.

Caroline pulled the bottle of wine from the cupboard, marched over to the table where he had seated himself, and read, "Gallo Hearty Burgundy. Too mundane for your tastes?"

He shrugged. "That's pretty cheap stuff. You ought to get yourself some—"

"Spare me the lecture on wine, please. It puts me to sleep at night and that's all I require of it."

He looked up at her. "You need wine to put you to sleep?"

"It relaxes me. I'm usually still keyed up by the time I go to bed."

"Hey, you know what *you* need, don't you?"

"No, but I'm sure I know what you *think* I need, and I don't want to hear about it." She poured out two glasses of wine and sat down, determined that he wasn't going to spoil her meal.

He gave her a wicked smile. "At least it's not white wine. I hate women who drink white wine."

Caroline helped herself to rare roast beef, several kinds of salad, and an onion bagel. "You certainly seem to categorize women."

"It's pretty hard not to."

"Easier than trying to see them as individuals, I suppose."

"Don't you categorize men?"

Caroline's brown eyes mocked him. "No. I think there's only one category of men."

"Oh, really? And what would that be?" he asked, his eyes challenging her.

She had to pause for a moment as the first word that came to mind was not fit to use at the dinner table. "Let's say I consider them all...expendable commodities."

"You categorize all men that way?"

"So far."

He wasn't looking amused at her philosophy of men. "Me included?"

"That's right," she said, taking a long drink of the wine and instantly feeling its soothing effects.

"You're a little hard on us males, you know that?"

She was too busy chewing to reply. She took another drink of wine under his watchful glance.

"I can't wait to see that stuff relax you," he murmured.

Caroline slammed down her fork. "Look, couldn't we just eat in peace?"

He gave her an innocent look. "Sure. Why not? So, Caroline, what do you do for fun?"

She eyed him suspiciously. "You're going to

have some smart remark about anything I say."

"No, really—what do you do with yourself when you're not working? Do you have a lot of friends?"

"I've only been in New York for a month. Anyway, my work takes up most of my time."

"Where did you live before?"

She resigned herself to his endless stream of personal questions. "Houston."

"I've never been to Texas. Is that where you grew up?"

"I was only in Houston for a couple of years. I grew up in California."

He gave her a big smile. "Ah—that explains it!"

"Explains what?"

"Everything. Your sunbathing on the fire escape, your indifference to whether your windows are locked, the way you dress. It's nice out there. I have a brother who lives in Irvine; do you know where that is?"

She began to relax. "Very well. I did my undergraduate work at the university there."

"And your graduate?"

"Harvard."

"I'm impressed."

"Like hell you are!"

Duffy's fork stopped dead halfway to his mouth. "What did you say?"

"You heard me. You're about as impressed by education as I am by your proclivity for putting people behind bars. And the cross-examination is over. If you feel a deep need for dinner conversation, you can talk about yourself."

"What would you like to know about me?"

"I wouldn't like to know anything about you, I just don't want to be questioned any longer. Particularly by someone who majored in psychology." Maybe, just maybe, that would shut him up.

It didn't. "You don't like psychology?" he asked.

"That's putting it mildly."

"Ever been in analysis?"

"No, and I never will be. And will you please knock off the questions? I'm beginning to feel you're putting me through some kind of therapy now."

"No dreams you'd like to tell me about?"

Caroline gave up and shoved the plate away from her. Many more dinners with him and she was sure she'd develop an ulcer. "I thought men liked to talk about themselves."

He gave her a beatific smile as though she had at last taken a personal interest in him. "I'm thirty, I own my own business, I went to N.Y.U., I own a house—"

"Spare me the job résumé," she interrupted him, afraid he was about to launch into his entire life story.

"For fun I relax women so they can sleep at night without benefit of wine..."

"You don't relax them—you put them to sleep with your incessant talking!"

Duffy laughed. "You're a pretty cool customer, you know that? Your apartment gets broken into and you don't even blink an eye."

She shrugged, finishing off her wine and pouring herself another glass.

"It didn't bother you at all?"

"Not really. Now if my office had been broken into, that would be a different matter."

Despite her vow not to clean up after him, she found the idea of clearing off the table preferable to remaining there and continuing the conversation.

"I guess that's why this place looks so impersonal," he mused. "You've probably got all your good stuff down at the office."

"What do you mean?"

"I don't see any pictures, knickknacks—not even a dead fern."

"The moose head is mine, and the map." And why did she keep letting him put her on the defensive. It was no business of his how she decorated, or didn't decorate, her apartment.

The more annoyed she became the more relaxed Duffy seemed to become. "Do you always have a map of the world on the wall?" he asked lazily, tilting the chair back on its legs, one foot hooked around the base of the table.

Caroline dumped the plates in the sink and gritted her teeth. "I like to know where I am."

"You're in New York."

"And you New Yorkers all think it's the center of the world!"

"Isn't it?" He got up and slowly walked over to where the map was fastened to the wall with thumbtacks. "It's just about in the center. Of course to be absolutely accurate, I guess you'd have to say...St. Louis is the center of the world."

Caroline put the deli containers in the brown bag and shoved it in the trash below the sink. "You wouldn't say that if the map hadn't been manufactured in this country," she remarked.

"Sure I would."

"On maps made in Europe, Europe is in the center. On maps made in Asia, Asia is in the center. On maps made—"

"I get the point! In other words, the center is arbitrary."

Caroline shrugged, sat down at the table, and poured herself more wine. Usually two glasses were her absolute limit, but she had had a wearing several hours and it wasn't over yet.

Duffy was now leaning against the map. "Do you want me to show you where you are?"

"I know where I am now that I have the map."

"You didn't know before?"

"Not precisely." She got up and walked over to where he was standing, motioning for him to stand aside. "You see, I thought it went New York, New Jersey, Pennsylvania, like that, right down the Eastern Seaboard, north to south," she said, pointing the way on the map. "Then I asked someone one day what that land was across the river, and he said it was New Jersey. And I knew I was looking west, and it didn't make sense. Do you see what I mean? I like to know exactly where I am in relation to the rest of the world.'' She went back to the table and sat down.

Duffy was looking dumbfounded. "I think you're a nut case,'' he said at last.

"And I think you have the average New Yorker's provincial view of the world.''

He sighed, running his hands through his curly hair. "You know, I can't understand why we're not hitting it off better.''

"Better? We're not hitting it off at all!''

"I'm afraid you're right,'' he said, opening his toolbox.

Duffy set to work installing the first windowgate on the living room window. Not finding the work entertaining to watch, Caroline opened her briefcase and took out her calculator and the papers she had brought home to work on. She was doing a financial report on a business her company was thinking of buying; based on her recommendation, they would decide whether or not to acquire it. She had been the financial whiz at the Houston office and had known it was only a matter of time until she was transferred to the corporate offices in New York. The next step would be vice-president in charge of finance and she was hopeful that would occur before her thirtieth birthday, which would be within the schedule she had set for herself. She had a degree in engineering, a master's in international marketing and her Ph.D. in finance, and once she was made vice-president she felt there'd be no stopping her.

At the moment, however, the consumption of wine seemed to be slowing her down. She knew it wasn't the calculator making all the mistakes so it must be her. She pushed the papers away, turned the calculator to ''off,'' and poured herself some more wine. Well, why not relax? She did it so seldom, and she really couldn't concentrate with Duffy in the room.

She lit a cigarette and looked over to where he was working. His back was to her and she noticed that he now had his shirt out of his pants and it must be undone judging by the way the air conditioner was blowing it back from his body. She'd better watch herself. Too much wine and she was liable to become mellow with this man, although she really didn't think Duffy had it in him to make her mellow. He was good-looking, even sexy, but that mouth of his really put her off. She preferred men who looked intelligent but kept their mouths shut.

Not the types at work, though. The men she worked with had never appealed to her. At least not physically. There was something so off-putting about their three-piece suits, their carefully styled hair, their corporate smiles. And even their scents. Particularly their scents. The mixture of Gentleman Givenchy and deodorant soap just didn't appeal to her. Duffy didn't smell like that. He smelled like sweat, a little salty... well, like a man.

She knew she'd been considered an enigma at the Houston office. Most of the unmarried executives, some of the married too, had tried to date her, but she had firmly said no to all of them. When she did start dating, it had been with one of the Houston Oilers, a muscular halfback with an easy smile, not much conversation, and a body she never tired of looking at. It had been Billy who had gotten her interested in lifting weights, taking her along with him to the gym and teaching her how to work out. She had loved him in her way, for the little boy he was at heart and for all the physical pleasure he had given her, but when she found out about her transfer she had had no regrets over saying good-bye.

He had asked her to marry him then, but she didn't think he was too broken up over her refusal. Anyway, she knew what Billy needed in a wife, and it wasn't a vice-president of an oil company. But they had had good times and she knew she was starting to feel the effects of not having a man around when she needed one. Like now. On the other hand, it was probably just the Gallo Hearty Burgundy that was making her feel that way.

Duffy turned around and caught her looking at him and she lowered her eyes. Not before she had gotten a good look at a muscular chest covered with black, curly hair, though. Maybe she had been wrong, maybe he did work out in a gym. Or maybe installing windowgates kept him in shape. And maybe she should quit thinking about Duffy's body, quit drinking so much wine, and just cool down!

"That guy across the street probably knows more about you than *I* do," said Duffy, breaking into her reverie.

"What guy across the street?"

He gave her an evil grin. "The one who watches you."

"That's just supposition on your part," said Caroline, having a little trouble pronouncing supposition. "There might not be anybody watching me."

Duffy chuckled. "He probably keeps a notebook on you. Knows what time you get up in the morning, what time you go to work, how often you entertain, what time you go to bed . . . whom you go to bed with."

Caroline smiled. "Sure, he probably does."

"Doesn't that worry you?"

"Not particularly."

"It should."

"If some guy's so bored he finds my life interesting, I really feel sorry for him."

"You don't have an interesting life?"

She gave him a condescending smile. "I find it interesting, I'm sure you wouldn't."

"Try me."

She lit a cigarette and watched him through the smoke. "Why this vicarious interest in my life?"

"You've got to be more interesting than you seem."

"Thanks a lot," she said, recognizing an insult when she heard one.

"Come on, Caroline—tell me about the men in your life."

"What men in my life?" Which was the problem, of course. If there was a current man in her life she wouldn't be sitting here having to listen to this. Or wanting to listen to this.

"There aren't any?" he asked, his tone disbelieving.

"No."

"Well, why not?"

"What is with you, Duffy? You really think men are some kind of necessity?"

"I think women are a necessity."

"That's your problem."

He looked around at her, his eyes gleaming. "I don't see it as a problem."

Caroline's calculating mind went into gear. This man was beginning to be a nuisance with all his personal questions. He obviously considered her some kind of oddity, probably a lot different than the women he saw socially. Well, why not live up to that image? Why not even elaborate on it? Why not, in fact, let him hear what he probably secretly believed female executives to be like? He was obviously a male chauvinist of the first degree and deserved everything he got!

"Look, I see men occasionally," said Caroline, her voice positively silky.

"Don't stop there!"

"You really want to know the truth, Duffy?"

"I swear to God!"

"I only see a man one time. After that the novelty's worn off and it's all downhill."

He turned around and stared at her in shock. "That's a hell of a lousy attitude."

She smiled sweetly. "I was sure you'd think so."

"You never have the urge to see a guy twice?"

She shook her head. "Never."

He gave a low whistle. "I'm glad you don't appeal to me—that attitude could be really demoralizing."

"I doubt you're that easily demoralized."

"You're not going to ask me why you don't appeal to me?"

"No."

"You know something, Caroline? You never answer the way a woman's supposed to."

"You've got women programmed?"

"I thought I had. You're making me reassess my thinking."

"Which is probably good for you."

"Glad you think so." He finished installing the windowgate, took a padlock out of the toolbox and snapped it in place, then stepped back to admire his work. "Nice, huh?"

"If you like cages," muttered Caroline.

"Time for a break," he said, sitting down across from her at the table. He poured himself some wine, poured her some more, then settled back in the chair.

She found her eyes drawn to the curly hair on his chest bared by the open shirt. Billy had been blond with only sparse hair on his muscular chest. She tried to remember whether she had ever known a man with much hair on his chest, but couldn't think of any. Not that her mind was all that clear from the inordinate amount of wine she had been drinking. Her eyes were drawn once more to his chest, and she wondered how that springy hair would feel rubbing against her naked body. Billy had had a powerful chest and arms and she had loved the feeling of being crushed against him, the illusion of being totally overpowered. She could see the sinewy strength in Duffy's arms where he had rolled the sleeves up and for a moment imagined being crushed in those arms, then shook her head, trying to clear it of unwanted thoughts.

She lifted her eyes and saw that Duffy was watching her, his dark eyes gleaming. "That wine relaxing you yet, Caroline?" he asked, his voice a lazy drawl.

She felt herself flush a little. "Not in any discernible way."

"Too bad," he said, pouring them each some more. He reached over and covered her hand with his, sending an electric charge through her body.

She quickly pulled her hand away. "Knock it off, Duffy," she said, anger and a little fear surfacing. Not fear of him, but fear that she reacted so strongly to his mere touch.

"Got a temper, have you? I should have suspected it with that red hair of yours."

"What?"

"Are you Irish?"

"No, I'm not Irish, and I don't have red hair. My hair's brown. Plain brown."

"Looks red to me."

"That's only because I've been in the sun a lot. It's usually brown."

"What are you if you're not Irish?"

"I'm American, if it's any business of yours."

"Your family, what are they?"

"American."

"You don't look Indian to me. You must have had ancestors who were something else."

"Way back they were English," she admitted.

"That figures. The Irish and the English never did get along."

"I can see why, now that I've met you," she said shortly. If her football player had talked this much she would never have tolerated him for so long.

He stood up. "One more windowgate to go, and then the lock on your door, and I'll be out of your life."

"And none too soon," muttered Caroline.

"Will you miss me when I'm gone?" he asked, beginning to fit the second window with the gate.

"You know, Duffy, you're just asking for it when you ask questions like that."

"I was hoping I'd get an honest answer this time."

She couldn't help laughing. "And what would you consider an honest answer?"

"I think you'll miss me."

"Well, think again. You're not my type, Duffy."

He turned to her. "Oh? What's your type?"

She thought for a second. "Clint Eastwood."

"Yeah, I guess the women go for him. Good-looking guy."

"It's not his looks I go for."

"Good actor too."

"Nor his acting ability."

He smiled. "Are you going to tell me what it is about him that appeals to you?"

"The way he keeps his mouth shut. I'll bet he could have installed my windowgates without saying a word!"

"How do you get to know someone if you don't talk?"

"I don't *want* to get to know you."

Without waiting for an answer, Caroline went into the bathroom and closed the door. She was feeling warm from the wine despite the air conditioning, and she splashed some cold water on her face. Her brown eyes were beginning to show signs of being bloodshot and she wasn't even all that steady on her feet. What was worse, despite his big mouth, Duffy was appealing more and more to her by the moment.

Which was due more to the fact that she hadn't been with a man for some time than it was to any personal charm on his part, she told herself, but the fact of the matter was he was the first man in New York to appeal to her at all, and there he was alone with her in her apartment and obviously interested in getting to know her. And if she didn't stop drinking that wine she was afraid she was going to end up doing something she'd regret in the morning.

It wasn't often that a man appealed to her, but when he did it was usually an instant attraction. And if there was one thing she wasn't, it was patient. On the other hand, while she was clearly physically attracted to Duffy, his incessant chatter was driving her berserk. If she required stimulating conversation she could get it at the office. With a man she just liked to relax, but with Duffy she felt she couldn't let her guard down for a moment. Damn the burglar! If it weren't for him she'd be at the gym working out instead of having to stay home and contend with Duffy's endless interrogation.

She went to the kitchen to make some coffee. When she was cold sober she'd reassess the situation. She put the water on to boil and saw that Duffy now had his shirt completely off. If she were to take her shirt off, no one would believe that she wasn't trying to incite him to passion. But it was perfectly all right for a man to remove his shirt, despite the fact that she couldn't take her eyes off the muscles in his back and shoulders and the way his torso narrowed down to a slim waist and hips. *Not a bad rear end either,* she thought, wondering if it would feel smooth and hard under her hands.

He turned around and caught her gaze, her eyes

not moving away in time. "Want to come over here and give me a hand?" he asked softly.

"No!"

"Afraid of my proximity?"

"No, of your overwhelming sex appeal," she said in her most sarcastic voice.

He laughed. "Am I making you nervous, Caroline?"

She turned off the whistling pot and poured it into a cup. "I'm beginning to think the mythical man across the street is less threatening than the wolf at my door."

She was just reaching into the cupboard to take out the jar of instant coffee when she heard him come up behind her. She whirled around, prepared to scream at him if necessary, but before she could even get her mouth open he had pinned her against the sink with his body and closed his hard mouth over hers.

Chapter Three

She tried to push him away, but he grasped the sink with his hands and held on tight, forcing his body even closer to hers. She tried moving her head but his head moved right along with hers, his lips still clinging to her mouth, a mouth that was compressed as tightly as she could manage to make it. She wanted to say something, to at least yell at him, but she was afraid if she opened her mouth at all he'd take it as an invitation.

She reached up to grab hold of his hair, managing to tug at one handful, but then his hands were on hers, and in a matter of moments she found both wrists pinned behind her back by one of his hands, the other one going around her shoulders and stilling the upper part of her body. She stamped hard on one of his feet, but since she was wearing soft running shoes it didn't seem to have any effect. And still he went on kissing her and she began to sense she was only putting up a fight because she felt it was required of her. If she were to really go along with her feelings, she would be kissing him back. However, it would never do to let Duffy know that; he was too self-confident as it was.

She became aware of his sweaty chest pressed tight against her breasts, the wetness dampening her shirt, and she could feel her nipples becoming erect, traitorously, refusing to obey the commands of her mind. The rest of her body felt as though it were dissolving, acting unaware of the fact that what she wanted most was to get out of this man's clutches. Her glaring at him had no effect as he had his eyes closed, which seemed ridiculous under the circumstances.

And then it dawned on her what was missing. Duffy was quiet. He wasn't talking. The room was suddenly so silent she could hear the hum of the air conditioner and even the sound of a television set in the next apartment.

What a relief it was, she thought, and then started to laugh. Her mouth opened and her laugh vibrated against his lips, but instead of taking advantage of it, he moved away from her, a look of annoyance on his face.

"You find it amusing?" he asked.

"Not at all," she said, getting her laughter under control. "I hardly find rape amusing."

"Rape? You consider a kiss rape?"

"I consider your forcing yourself upon me rape, yes."

He stood back from her, his blue eyes darkening. "Burglarized and raped in one day. Maybe you'd better call the police again."

She knew she was being unfair. If she hadn't been so friendly to him all evening it wouldn't have happened. "I guess it wasn't exactly rape," she admitted.

"As far as I'm concerned, it wasn't even a kiss," he said, going back to his work at the window.

"That's because it wasn't mutual!"

"I thought women liked aggressive men."

"I don't!"

"No, not you. I should have figured you to be different. Big female executive—you probably like to make the first move, right?"

"Let's just forget it, Duffy. Would you like some coffee?"

"You probably ask the man out, pay for the date, and call the shots. Am I right?"

"I'm not going to discuss it. Do you want some coffee or not?"

"You drink it. I don't need sobering up."

Caroline sat down at the table with her coffee and lit a cigarette. Truthfully she liked aggressive men and thought there were too few of them around. Most of the men she met seemed intimidated by her, by her job, her education and the fact that she usually made more money than they did. Billy hadn't been and Duffy didn't seem to be, and that was rare in a man. She knew she was strong herself and couldn't tolerate weakness in a man. She wanted men to treat her as an equal, but she wanted to be able to treat them that way, too, and it seemed that these days the only strong people she met were women.

Duffy had gone several minutes without speaking, which must mean he was mad at her. He was a little too nosy and he asked far too many questions, but she liked the way he stood up to her and gave her back as good as she gave him. Most men would have folded by now. It wouldn't hurt to needle him a little more, reinforce his image, albeit wrong, of the hard-nosed businesswoman.

"What's the matter, Duffy, you used to seducing your customers?"

"Only the female ones." Well, he hadn't permanently lost his voice.

"Are you serious?" Perhaps it wasn't her, maybe he made passes at every woman he met.

"There are a lot of lonely ladies around."

"I don't believe you."

He turned around and grinned at her and there was something about that grin she didn't like. "Do you know Mrs. Jacobson in Three B? Or Carol McFadden in Five F? And there's your next door neighbor—I think her name was Marylou. And that's just this building."

"You are such a liar!"

"And, of course, your super—Chloe."

Suddenly there was a ring of truth to his words and she found herself holding her breath at the mention of Chloe's name. And an unfamiliar sensation came over her, a sensation she could only term as jealousy. She wondered why she should care that maybe he had been with Chloe. They'd probably be great together—both of them crazy! "You and Chloe?" she asked in a small voice.

"Ah, so you're finally getting curious about me?" he asked, his voice lightening. "Do I detect a vicarious interest?"

"You do not!"

He chuckled. "I was only kidding. Chloe and I are good friends, that's all. And I really don't generally believe in mixing business with pleasure. Anyway, Caroline, you shouldn't get the idea that just because you choose to live without sex, everyone in New York is following your example."

"I never said I was living without sex," she said, hoping to get a rise out of him.

"No, that's right, it's not sex you do without, it's romance. Love. One time only, right?"

"Absolutely," she said sweetly.

"What's the matter with you, anyway? Don't you want to meet some nice guy, fall in love . . ."

"No."

"Why not? Can you tell me that?"

"I don't want to be trapped."

"You think love is a trap?"

"It's the most effective way to lose your freedom that I know of," she said vehemently, now on a subject dear to her heart.

"You really think you're free, don't you?"

"I am free."

"You're tied to your job—"

"I could quit it tomorrow."

"Caroline, nobody's really free."

"That's where you're wrong. I'm free to do whatever I want—exactly what I want. If I feel like quitting my job I can, if I want to get out of New York I'll move—"

"And if you want to fall in love?"

"But you see, I don't want to. I don't romanticize things, Duffy. I don't see sex as love or love as something leading to marriage. I view sex as a pleasurable activity, love as a transitory state, and marriage as a prison."

"It wouldn't have to be a prison." He had stopped all pretense at work and was leaning back against the window.

"What about you? You don't work for anyone else and you're not married—I don't see you relinquishing your freedom."

"I'm a man."

"What's that supposed to mean?"

"Men are just naturally more independent."

"Oh, baloney!"

"I'm not afraid of marriage—I just haven't met anyone I want to marry."

"I'm not afraid of it either—it just doesn't interest me."

He gave her a condescending look. "I guess you haven't met the right person yet either."

That infuriated her, being exactly what her mother always said to her. "Duffy, there is no right person."

"Don't be so sure," he said, giving her his sexy smile.

She saw his look and laughed. "I suppose you think it's you, is that it, Duffy? Don't make me laugh!"

"The wine sure didn't relax that nasty tongue of yours," he said.

"You think I'm nasty?"

"You think you're Miss Sweetness and Light?"

"I can be much worse than this. I've been pretty polite to you."

"God help the guys you're impolite to!"

"I thought you could take it. You didn't exactly walk in here as your friendly neighborhood locksmith. You didn't even know me and the first words out of your mouth were some smart remark."

He walked over to the table and sat down beside her. "That's what's called instant attraction, Caroline."

"I call it being rude!"

"No," he said, shaking his head. "If you had thought that you would have thrown me right out. Admit it, sparks were flying between us the moment we met. You haven't been any more indifferent to me than I have to you. It's electric—I can feel it now sitting next to you."

That was a line of conversation she didn't want to pursue. "Next time I'll throw you out."

"There won't be a next time. I defy anyone to break into this place when I'm done with it."

"When *are* you going to be done with it?"

He put his hand over hers. "You in a hurry for me to leave?".

She left her hand there, trying to prove she felt no reaction at all. "I just asked a simple question."

"If you're hoping to get rid of me soon, abandon all hope. I'm almost through with the gate, but I still have the front door to do."

"How long do you think—"

"Don't try to rush me; I refuse to do sloppy work." He reached over and put his hand on the back of her neck, the fingers softly caressing it.

She sat stunned by the force of feelings washing over her at his touch. She could feel each individual callused finger against her soft skin, could feel her body tensing, then tingling all over from the sheer eroticism of the gesture. He was watching her, probably judging her reaction, and she tried to remain cool, indifferent to whatever his fingers might be doing. She wanted to reach out and touch his muscular arm, his hard chest, and it took all her self-control not to do so. She wanted him at that moment, wanted him more than she could ever remember wanting a man. His pure sexuality was overwhelming her and she knew that if he made a move at the moment she wouldn't be able to resist it.

Finally, as though satisfied by what he had seen on her face, he removed his hand and stood up. "Time to get back to work," he said, then left her sitting there trembling as he returned to finish the window.

She took a sip of the wine and lit a cigarette, trying to still her nerves. She tried to think back to Billy and how he had made her feel. He had gradually loosened her up, as she recalled, made her feel at ease with her own sexuality, but she couldn't remember ever feeling as turned on by him as she did by Duffy when he had merely put his hand on her neck. Maybe it was the wine. Maybe it was all the mental sparring that had come before. Whatever it was it was completely unnerving her.

"You okay?" asked Duffy, his back to her as he put the finishing touches on the windowgate.

She swallowed. "Of course I'm okay," she said, her voice cracking a little. If she didn't watch it she was going to demolish her image of the cool female executive.

"You don't have to worry," he said casually. "I'm not going to do anything to make you yell rape again."

"I didn't yell rape."

"You certainly inferred it."

Did that mean that it was over? That he was going to give up after one aborted attempt at a kiss? She had thought he was more aggressive than that, but perhaps she was wrong. Or maybe he really did believe she liked to make the first move, call the shots. And to be honest, maybe he was right about that. She pretty much did get her own way with men, in her own time. If she had felt like kissing him, she certainly wouldn't have given up so easily.

She finished the glass of wine and stubbed out her cigarette. *Face it, Caroline,* she told herself. *It's been a long time since Billy and you want this man. And it certainly doesn't appear that he would turn you down. Everyone else these days has an occasional one-night stand, probably more than occasionally. You'll never have to see him again after tonight. But for now, just for once, why not go with your feelings? It would be dishonest not to.*

She saw that he had finished with the window and was now putting the padlock on and snapping it shut. She stood up and walked a little unsteadily to the window, reaching out and taking hold of the bars in her hands. They were firmly attached and didn't give.

"How do you like them?" he asked, taking a step back to admire his work.

She sat down on the windowsill and leaned back against the bars. "I feel like I'm a prisoner," she murmured as his body moved in front of her. His chest was gleaming with sweat and despite the air conditioning she felt very warm herself.

"They should make you feel safe," he said softly, his eyes making contact with hers and defying her to look away.

Her mouth felt dry and she moved her tongue out to wet her lips. As though it had a will of its own, one of her hands touched his chest, feeling the texture of the wet, crinkly hair, then the muscles beneath it. She traced the contours of his chest down to where the line of hair disappeared into his pants, then with a shudder sank back against the bars on the window.

Their eyes were still locked and his seemed to be turning a darker and darker blue. "Don't start something you don't mean to finish," he warned her, his voice dangerous.

She tried to speak but no words came, and then she was standing up and pressing her body against his as his arms went around her, pinning her in their viselike grip. His mouth roughly attacked the mouth she lifted to him, and she could feel her lips being bruised by his merciless kiss. He was strong, as strong as Billy, and much rougher than Billy had been. Billy had been boyish, an overgrown kid playing at love, but with Duffy she felt she was being kissed by a man. She liked the sense of being overpowered by him, of being at his mercy, although she knew full well it had been her move that had precipitated their now being locked in an embrace.

His rough chin was rubbing the skin on her own as his mouth moved back and forth against her lips, his wet tongue moistening them from time to time. She parted her lips to let his tongue gain access to her mouth, and it immediately thrust inside, filling her mouth with its driving force. She tasted his tongue, then moved her own into his mouth, doing her own explorations as her arms moved to encircle him. She could feel the muscles in his shoulders and back, his biceps bulging from the force with which he was holding her to him.

She began imperceptibly to move her breasts back and forth against his chest, inflaming herself to the point where she knew she'd have trouble standing if he were to let go of her. She felt weak all over, weak and yet sexually alive in every nerve in her body. It couldn't just be the wine; she had consumed wine on many occasions without this result. It had to be Duffy. He was right when he said there had been sparks between them since they met. And those sparks were gradually turning a physical attraction into a sexual inferno that showed no signs of burning out.

His hands moved down to her buttocks, moving her closer to him until she felt him pressed against her and she knew he was as excited as she was. A moan escaped his lips, and then his hand was on her breast, his thumb and forefinger squeezing her taut nipple. She was moving against him, impatient with the kissing now, wanting him to make love to her. She wanted his naked body against her own, to arrive at that place where she could no longer think, no longer make decisions.

She broke off the kiss, staring intently into his surprised eyes. "Make love to me, Duffy," she said softly.

His hand was still on her breast, caressing the nipple. "Don't be in such a hurry," he murmured, leaning down to kiss her once again.

She moved her head to the side, avoiding his kiss. "I want to make love now."

He looked amused. "Can we go into the bedroom or do you prefer making love in front of the window?''

She went into the bedroom, turning on the light and quickly shedding her clothes. When she was naked she turned and saw him leaning against the bedroom door watching her.

He drew in his breath at the sight of her body and took a step toward her. She reached for his pants and unbuckled the belt, then unzipped them and let them fall to his feet. He sat down on the side of he bed and slowly removed his shoes and socks, then stood up to pull down his briefs.

When he was naked, he picked her up and tossed her on the bed. "You really don't have much patience, do you?" he asked as she held out her arms to him.

"Don't talk, Duffy, just make love to me," she said.

He got on the bed and straddled her, his mouth once more seeking hers. She wrapped her legs around him and pulled him close against her, urging him on. When he entered her she sighed, a smile of satisfaction lighting up her face, and he broke off the kiss to raise himself on his elbows to look down at her. "You are so beautiful," he murmured, one hand brushing the damp hair back off her face.

"Don't stop, Duffy," she said, seeing his eyes once again darken at her command. She raised her body to meet his, and then he was thrusting inside her, sending the world crashing around her as she felt herself quickly being lifted into the heights. She could never remember feeling this so quickly, so effortlessly, and even as she tried to analyze it she felt herself being swept beyond being able to even think coherently. Suddenly she was no mind and all sensation, every part of her body consumed with passion.

He made love to her forcefully, driving her eager body against the mattress again and again, causing her to cry out with pleasure as she reached the heights and then exploded with ecstasy, cascading over the sides only to be lifted up once again. And still he continued, never seeming to tire, until she felt so weakened she couldn't even summon the strength to cry out, "No more."

When he finally reached his own explosive point and then lowered his body on top of hers, she clung to him, her lips seeking his neck, his ear, and then his face. He rolled over beside her, one arm beneath her neck, the other flung across her waist while they both got their breathing under control.

He was strangely silent and she was grateful for this, not wanting to hear the kind of instant replay in words that had always been Billy's habit. After a while he leaned over and kissed her softly on the lips, then got off the bed and she watched as he put on his clothes and went back to the living room.

She finally sat up on the side of the bed feeling weak all over. She went into the bathroom, took a warm shower, then put on a terry-cloth robe hanging on the back of the door. He had seen her naked now; she didn't feel it was necessary to get fully clothed again. Anyway, he would be leaving soon and she would go right to bed.

As she opened the bathroom door and prepared to enter the living room, the enormity of what she had done began to sink in. She had made love to a man she barely knew; had even perhaps seduced him. A man she had no intention of ever seeing again. She waited for the feelings of guilt she was sure would come, but none came. Instead she felt good about it. It had felt right to her at the time and it still felt right. In fact she could never remember feeling better. Maybe she was becoming more modern in her outlook than she had been aware of. Maybe she was capable of one-night stands and didn't know it. It was something to think about, but not now. Tomorrow she would analyze what she had done and come to some decision about it.

She went into the kitchen and put on some water for coffee. She didn't think she'd need any more wine in order to sleep tonight.

"You're really incredible, you know that?" said Duffy, at work on installing the lock in the front door.

She had been hoping the rest of the time he was there would pass in relative silence. "I can live without a recap, Duffy," she said shortly.

He smiled at her. "That would take too long. Just a compliment, that's all. Incidentally, this is the safest lock on the market. You have to use the key to get out as well as get in. That way you'll never lock yourself out."

"How much longer will you be?" she asked, wanting nothing so much now as to get to bed and sleep.

"Not long. You eager to get rid of me?"

"I'm just tired."

"Tomorrow's Saturday, you can sleep," he said.

The pot began to whistle and she made herself a cup of coffee and settled down on the couch with it.

"What if I stayed closed tomorrow? We could go for a drive; I'll show you my house. Staten Island's pretty this time of the year and cooler than the city. Kind of quiet and peaceful, I think you'd like it."

"If I liked 'quiet and peaceful' I wouldn't be living in the city."

"Don't you ever get tired of it? Want to get away for a while?"

"I guess I haven't been here long enough to get tired of it. When I do, I'll move."

"Just like that?"

"Just like that."

He was silent for a moment, then, "How about dinner tomorrow night?"

"What?"

"Dinner. You know—like eating. There's a good French restaurant over on Second Avenue I think you'd like. I'll treat you to something a little better than Gallo."

Caroline scalded her tongue on the coffee and

gave him an annoyed look. Why did he have to spoil everything now by all that chattering. "No thanks."

"Why not? You got other plans?"

"No. No other plans."

"You'd rather do something else? Just name it and we'll do it."

Caroline settled back on the couch, wrapping her robe more tightly around her. She could still feel her skin tingling in all the places he had touched her, but she was finding his voice abrasive. "Duffy, I don't think you quite understood me."

"Oh, come on," he said impatiently, "you weren't serious about that one-time-only business."

"I certainly was." She hadn't been at the time, but then it had only been a theory she had never put to practice. Now she was definitely serious.

He had turned around now, lock in hand, and was looking at her in disbelief. "Are you telling me you're just going to let me walk out of here and never see me again? After what we just did?"

"I told you how it was."

"Yeah, but I didn't believe you."

"You should have. I don't play games, Duffy."

"Maybe not the normal ones—just perverse ones of your own!" He was beginning to sound angry.

"I don't have time for entanglements," she told him airily.

"Since when does dinner constitute an entanglement?"

"Tonight was lovely, Duffy, but that's it!"

"Like hell it is!" He slammed the lock in the door and began to screw it in.

She began to wonder if she was being smart making him so angry when she was all alone with him. After all, how much did she really know about him? On the other hand, she had been to bed with him so she felt she knew him fairly well. And it was her experience that the best way to get rid of a man was to make him angry at her.

"So, it's one-night stands only with you, huh? That's all you go in for?"

"I don't consider them one-night stands," said Caroline, improvising as she went along.

"Yeah? Well, just what's your definition of a one-night stand?"

She thought about that for a moment. "When you pick up a guy in a singles' bar, take him home with you and never even ask his name."

"And what do you call what *you* do?"

"Brief encounters," she said with a chuckle. She didn't know where the phrase had come from, but it sounded perfect.

"You think that makes it sound more romantic? *Brief encounters*?" His sarcasm was cutting.

"The first night with anyone could turn into a one-night stand if it doesn't work out," she rationalized.

"And your 'brief encounters' just never happen to work out, is that it?"

She laughed. "I guess not."

"You really find it amusing, don't you? I think you're sick. I know you don't like shrinks, but you've really got a problem."

Caroline was trying her best to control the laughter welling up inside her. She had certainly tried the right tack with Duffy. At this rate she was sure she'd never be bothered by him again. "I don't consider it a problem," she told him.

"How many men have you gone through, anyway?"

"Thousands," she said, then couldn't stop the laugh that erupted. Obviously he was willing to believe the very worst about her, she must have played the part well. Conversely, she guessed he had every reason to believe it since it was happening to him. So maybe it did make it true about her. At least now. Somehow she didn't like that idea very much.

"You really think you're funny, don't you?"

"Come on, Duffy, haven't you ever had a one-night stand?"

"You mean before tonight?"

"Yes."

"Not intentionally. I mean you're right, sometimes it works out that way, but I'm always sorry when that happens."

She shrugged. "You probably expect too much."

He finished installing the lock and now leaned against the door. "How often do you have these... brief encounters."

She thought quickly. "Fortnightly."

"What's that, every two weeks?"

She nodded.

"You *schedule* it?" he asked incredulously.

"Certainly I schedule it. I find that extending good business practices over into my personal life provides me with maximum efficiency."

"You actually schedule your sex?"

"Why not? I schedule everything else. I run six miles every morning between seven fifteen and eight. I eat lunch every day at one, I—"

"You *schedule* your *sex*?"

"The first and third Fridays of every month," she said, having done the quick calculation in her head.

He paused, assessing her for a moment. She could almost feel him trying to rein in his anger. "*This* is the third Friday of the month."

She gave a nervous giggle. "That's right." She got up off the couch and went over to the table where he had put his estimate and began to check the figures with her calculator.

He walked over and stared down at her, his face betraying no emotion. "What are you doing?"

"Just checking your arithmetic."

"You don't trust my arithmetic?"

"People make mistakes."

"People using calculators make mistakes, too. Well? Did I make a mistake?"

"Not this time."

"I wouldn't be so sure," he muttered.

"Will you take a check? Although you know, it

probably would have been cheaper and simpler just to install a burglar alarm."

"They're no good. They go off all the time and no one pays any attention to them."

He was saying the words but she could tell he was almost too angry to speak. Well, too bad. Men did it to women all the time, didn't they?

She wrote out a check and handed it to him. "Thanks. I appreciate your doing it tonight."

"Not enough for an encore though, I guess."

She could feel herself flush. "I was talking about the locks."

"Yeah, I know."

He started to put his tools away in his tool chest and she began to feel a little sorry that they couldn't at least part friends. "Would you like a cup of coffee before you go?" she asked, trying to make her voice sound friendly and impersonal at the same time.

"No thanks. It has been a pleasure, Caroline." He headed for the front door and she got up and followed him.

Once at the door he turned around and confronted her. "You're just going to stand there coolly and say good-bye to me, aren't you? No kiss. No 'Why don't you call me, Duffy.'"

"Good-bye, Duffy."

He opened the door, then turned to look down at her. "You know something, Caroline? You wouldn't know the right man if he came along. You go through men so fast you wouldn't have time to recognize him." He went out the door slamming it behind him.

"Not so fast I didn't recognize you weren't the right one!" she yelled through the door. Then, afraid he hadn't heard her and absolutely determined to have the final word with him this time, she turned the handle to open the door. It turned, but the door didn't open.

He was probably in the lobby already anyway. She went over to the window, thinking she'd open it and yell down the words when he appeared on the street. Not very dignified behavior, but then she had lacked dignity most of the night.

She looked around to see where he had put the keys to the windowgates, but didn't see them. In fact she didn't see any keys anywhere. And hadn't he said she would need a key in order to get out as well as in?

Frantically now, she began to search the apartment, trying to find the keys she was certain were not there. She finally gave up, coming to the only conclusion she could come to. He had locked her in. Whether on purpose or not, the results were the same.

She was a prisoner in her own apartment!

Chapter Four

Caroline's first inclination was to kick in the front door. On second thought, she realized she was barefoot and desisted. Of course there was always the possibility that Duffy had inadvertently locked her in and not left the keys. A slight possibility, to be sure, but he had left angry and probably wasn't thinking straight.

On the other hand, she wouldn't put it past him to deliberately lock her in as a direct result of her one-time-only policy. He might have figured that if she wouldn't see him again of her own volition, he'd make very certain she'd have to see him again. This was the kind of devious thinking she simply wouldn't tolerate. She liked to be in control of a situation, and being locked in her own apartment deprived her of that.

She had options, of course. For one, she could always call the police. The thought of having to explain to the police that on the same day she was robbed the local locksmith had locked her in her apartment would be highly embarrassing. They would probably think it was all one big mistake, and she couldn't disabuse them of that notion and press any kind of criminal charges against Duffy without the story coming out of the intimate encounter they had had. Which would be just the kind of human interest story the newspapers would probably pick up and splash all over the front pages of their questionable papers. And it just wouldn't do for a potential vice-president to get that kind of publicity. No, the police were out.

Another locksmith? She looked in the Yellow Pages and saw that several offered emergency twenty-four-hour service. She could have the job done right this time and stop payment on the check to Duffy.

She called one of the locksmiths listed, got an answering service, and was called back a few minutes later only to be told that an emergency constituted being locked out, not in, and that he would come over in the morning. Caroline told him no thank you. By morning she was sure Duffy would return and she wouldn't need another locksmith.

Still, she didn't fancy being locked in all night. What if there were a fire in the building? She looked up Chloe's number in the book and dialed. A sleepy voice answered and Caroline realized it was almost two in the morning, not really a civilized hour in which to be making phone calls.

"This is Caroline Hart in Four A," she identified herself. "I'm locked in."

There was a pause. "Locked in?"

"Yes."

Another pause. "Did you call Duffy like I suggested?"

"He's the one who locked me in."

"I think this must be a dream," she heard Chloe murmur and was afraid her super was going to hang up on her.

"It's not a dream, Chloe," she said loudly. "I'm locked in my apartment and I think he did it deliberately."

"Duffy wouldn't do something like that. Did you call him?"

Caroline sighed. "The light's out in his shop, he must be on his way home to Staten Island."

"Look, I'll call him in the morning for you."

"What if there's a fire during the night?" Caroline practically yelled.

"Stay calm," advised Chloe. "I'll be right up."

Caroline, who felt exceedingly calm despite the situation, wondered what Chloe expected to do. Read her tea leaves through the door, perhaps? She went in the kitchen and put on some water to boil. This was definitely going to be a night for black coffee.

Moments later she heard a knock at her door. She went over to the door and leaned her ear against it. "Is that you, Chloe?"

"I'll have it unlocked in a minute," Chloe assured her.

Had she gotten hold of Duffy for the key? Was

she going to use tools to remove the lock? Or perhaps she knew some kind of astrological mumbo jumbo that made locks suddenly open. .

She made two cups of coffee in case Chloe drank something besides herbal tea, and was just sitting down at the table when the door opened and Chloe, clad only in a pink T-shirt that reached to her knees, walked in the door. She was a dead ringer for Little Orphan Annie.

Chloe left the door ajar and joined Caroline at the table. "Piece of cake," she said, a delighted grin on her face.

"Duffy swore you couldn't open that lock with a credit card," said Caroline.

"I didn't use a credit card; I used a hairpin."

"So much for pick-proof locks."

"It wasn't all that easy," said Chloe, "but I'm pretty good at it. When tenants forget their keys I can always open the door for them." She was looking at the windowgates. "He seemed to make you secure in here. So what happened, he forget to leave the keys?"

"That's a possibility," Caroline conceded, "although I tend to the theory that it was deliberate."

"Why would Duffy deliberately lock you in?"

"Because he's a nut, that's why."

"Incidentally, that nut and you have a lot in common," said Chloe, giving her a wink from one green eye that still bore traces of eye shadow.

Caroline offered sugar and cream, which Chloe

declined. "I assure you, Mr. Duffy and I have nothing in common." She wondered where her super could have got such a notion.

"The stars never lie," Chloe intoned.

"I beg your pardon?"

"I did your chart and it was just incredible. I knew it reminded me of something and then some sixth sense I have at times told me to look at the copy of Duffy's chart. I got it out of my files, placed it next to yours, and *voila*—absolutely complementary! If ever two people were meant for each other, it's you and Duffy." She sat back, giving Caroline the kind of smug smile she would expect from a Cheshire cat.

All of which reinforced Caroline's views on astrology. Caroline offered Chloe a cigarette, took one herself, then lit them both. "I read your column, Chloe, and really enjoyed it. But as for believing any of that, forget it!"

"The column wasn't meant to be believed, it's more of a parody of astrological columns. But charts are another thing entirely. Listen, if there wasn't anything to it there wouldn't be so many people who believed in it."

Which was about as illogical an argument as Caroline had ever heard. "There was a time a lot of people believed the world to be flat. Was there something to that?"

Chloe grinned. "Well, I just happen to belong to the Flat Earth Society."

Caroline was not about to be drawn into an argument about that. At least not at two o'clock in the morning.

"Getting back to the subject at hand," said Chloe, "just what makes you think Duffy locked you in on purpose?"

"He was angry about something and I think he did it just to teach me some kind of lesson."

"Why would he be angry? He seems to have sold you enough stuff. Did you refuse to pay him or something?"

"No. I wrote him a check. It was something... personal."

Chloe lifted an inquisitive brow. "Personal?"

"He didn't seem to care for my attitude toward men," said Caroline, wondering why she was answering any of Chloe's questions. It wasn't like her to confide in another woman, but this one was so persistent.

Chloe's eyes widened with interest. "Your attitude toward men in general or Duffy in particular?"

"Both."

Chloe gave her a knowing look. "Ah ha! So I was right. Duffy, whom I've always found to be very perceptive, sensed at once that you two were perfect for each other, then couldn't understand it when you didn't feel the same. Which would explain perfectly why he locked you in. It was really a romantic gesture when you think of it."

Caroline thought of it. Heretofore she had never inspired romantic gestures in men, but put in that context locking her in did have a sort of appeal, nutty as it was.

"Rather like locking a princess in a tower to keep her pure," Chloe was now rhapsodizing, clearly caught up in the romantic aspect of the situation.

"You're assuming, of course, that I was pure to begin with," said Caroline.

"On the contrary, I never assume anyone over eighteen is pure, but in your case... well, there is something rather forbidding about you, you know."

"Unfortunately, Duffy didn't seem to think so."

Chloe choked on the smoke she had been inhaling and it was moments before she could speak. "You mean he made a move on you?"

Caroline started to answer, then instead summoned up her forbidding manner that Chloe had previously noted. "I'd really rather not discuss it," she said coolly.

But Chloe was having none of that. "You can't say that much and then stop," she protested. "If you don't tell me, I'll just think the very worst."

Since "the very worst" was exactly what happened, Caroline was at a loss over what to say. "Think what you want," she finally muttered.

"No. I don't believe it. Not Duffy. He would never force his attentions on a woman, not that I think he's ever had to. I've never met a woman yet who hasn't fallen for those Irish looks of his."

Caroline imagined a whole stream of women following Duffy around, no doubt thrusting their phone numbers at him. Then reality returned. "It's not his looks I object to," she said, "it's his big mouth."

"He does talk a lot," Chloe conceded, "but he's intelligent and I've always found him interesting. Anyway, I can keep up my end of the conversation with him anytime."

Caroline was sure of it.

"Besides, I've always found Duffy a perfect gentleman." She paused, obviously waiting for a reaction, then continued when one wasn't forthcoming. "What did he do to you?"

"I'd really rather not talk about it."

Chloe reached for Caroline's pack of cigarettes, lit one, and leaned back in her chair. "I'm not leaving until I hear every detail. Listen, I feel like I've got a responsibility in this—I was the one who told you to call him, if you remember. Come on, you're obviously harboring hostile feelings about him and it will help you to get them out in the open.

Was everyone in the neighborhood an amateur shrink? she wondered. Somehow the entire evening now began to seem to Caroline like something that happened in another time and to someone else. It lacked any reality at the moment at all and she could hardly believe now that any of it had indeed occurred.

She began to relate the evening to Chloe and found her a receptive audience. She laughed at times, occasionally interspersed a question, and was a totally captive listener. When she was finished, down to the final detail of Duffy walking out and leaving her locked in, Chloe burst out laughing.

"This is better than television," she enthused, looking at Caroline with undisguised admiration. "It's a wonder you didn't drive the poor man right round the bend!"

"I may have," admitted Caroline.

"I must remember that one-time-only policy for future reference. I bet that would effectively put to an end any ideas of a one-night stand a man might have."

"No doubt," said Caroline.

"But didn't you feel anything at all for Duffy? Were you just using the poor man?"

"Yes, two things: a strong repulsion and an equally strong physical attraction."

"That's incredible," breathed Chloe.

"Of course I wouldn't have done it if I had thought I'd have to see him again. I've never done that before, Chloe, I swear—but I just couldn't seem to resist the temptation."

"And of course there was also the strong physical attraction."

"I certainly couldn't have done it without that. My first one-night stand. That's rather a milestone, isn't it?"

"A giant step for women's liberation," agreed Chloe. "Is that Gallo Hearty Burgundy I see over there?"

Caroline nodded.

"I think we should have a drink to your first one-night stand. Anyway, I'm wide awake now."

Caroline was too, so she got them each a glass and poured them both some wine. It was probably the only thing that would help her sleep at this point. She was as amazed at her confession to Chloe as she had been over what she'd done with Duffy. Clearly it had not been her day.

They drank their wine in silence for a few minutes, then when Caroline poured them each some more, Chloe finally spoke up again.

"There's just one thing I don't understand. If there's a strong physical attraction, why don't you want to see him again?"

"I don't like him."

"How can you have a strong physical attraction for someone you don't like?"

"That's what I've been asking myself."

"My theory of love," said Chloe, "is that it's ninety-nine percent physical attraction."

"What's the other one percent?"

"A nice body."

The wine spluttered out of Caroline's mouth as she burst out laughing. "If that were true, Chloe, I'd be in love," she finally managed to say.

"Yeah, Duffy's got a nice body," Chloe agreed. "At least what I've seen of him in clothes, you understand."

"Luckily, however, that's not my theory of love," said Caroline.

"What's yours?"

"I've never really formulated it before."

"Try now."

"I guess I'd have to say fifty percent would be a meeting of minds, probably twenty-five percent for mutual interests..."

"And the other twenty-five percent?"

"I suppose physical attraction."

"I think your percentages are all off," said Chloe. "Have you ever been in love?"

"You mean wildly and passionately?"

Chloe nodded.

"I don't think so."

"Have you ever been physically attracted?"

"Oh, yes."

"Well, I think the 'wildly and passionately' you talk about is simply physical attraction. I think that's basically what love is."

"Then animals would fall in love."

"I think they do."

"I think you're nuts!"

"Well, I'll tell you what I think. I think the stars are right and you and Duffy are going to turn out to be the great romance of the century. The only problem is, you might not be aware of it. What a waste."

It was a vicious circle, Caroline was thinking. First she needed coffee in order to sober up, then she needed wine to counteract the effects of the caffeine and go to sleep, now she was once again feeling in need of coffee. She must be drunk; Chloe was beginning to make great sense to her.

Tired of spending so long sitting in the hard chair, she got up, went over to the couch, then settled down on the carpeted floor, leaning her head back against the couch. Chloe joined her.

"I suppose we ought to get some sleep," said Caroline.

Chloe nodded sleepily in agreement.

They sat in companionable silence for a while, and then Chloe asked, "If this was a movie, what do you think would happen next?"

"You mean the whole thing with Duffy?"

"Yeah."

"I guess it would depend on what kind of movie it was."

"I was thinking of a romantic comedy."

"You watch old movies on television?" Caroline asked her.

"All the time. Do you?"

"Ummm. Well, if this was a Doris Day/Rock Hudson kind of movie, first of all, I'd still be pure. He'd show up tomorrow, we'd clown around for a few more scenes, and in the end we'd wind up married."

"Sounds good to me," said Chloe.

"Not to me! However, if it was one of those old Katherine Hepburn/Spencer Tracy movies, I'd probably get revenge on him."

"What kind of revenge?"

Caroline thought about it for a moment. "Maybe when he walked in tomorrow I'd give him a ka-rate chop, tie him up, and let him feel what it's like to be a prisoner."

"You'd still wind up married in the end."

"Maybe, but it wouldn't be so boring in be-tween."

"Is that what you're going to do when Duffy shows up? Give him a karate chop?"

"I don't know any karate. Do you?"

"No."

"On the other hand, it could be a thriller, maybe with Audrey Hepburn and one of those English ac-tors. In which case, Duffy would be the weirdo who broke into my apartment in the first place in order to get me to call his shop, then when he came back he'd probably torture me."

"And the valiant super would come to your res-cue."

"Only the super would be a man."

"And you'd end up marrying him."

Caroline sighed. "Old movies never have satis-fying endings. Why did they always get married?"

"I think that was known as a 'happy ending.'"

Chloe dragged herself up from the floor. "If I don't go downstairs now, I'm going to fall asleep here. What *are* you going to do when he shows up?"

"I'm too tired to think about it now. My inclina-tion would be not to speak to him at all, but Duffy talks so much he probably wouldn't even notice. I don't know; I'll think about it in the morning."

She didn't even get up as Chloe headed for the door and they exchanged good nights. It was only after the door had closed after her, and Caroline finally got up off the floor, that she realized that once more she was locked in her apartment. For the moment, though, that didn't seem to bother her.

Chapter Five

Caroline found herself awake at seven and unable to get back to sleep. She went into the bathroom and turned on the radio. The middle of September already and the weather was still in the nineties and humid. She had thought New York would be cooler than Houston, but so far it had been equally as hot and humid ever since she had arrived.

She took a shower and washed her hair, then blew it dry before fastening it into a ponytail. She dressed in running shorts and a tank top, then stripped the bed, putting the sheets and pillowcases into her laundry bag to drop off on the way to the gym. There was the faint smell of Duffy on the sheets, but she didn't need that to remind her of him. Ever since she woke up she'd been listening for the sound of his entering her apartment.

She put on water to boil for coffee, then emptied the ashtrays and washed the wineglasses. When she finally sat down at the table with her cup of coffee she was feeling eminently cool and calm.

When Duffy arrived she wouldn't even give him the satisfaction of admitting she had known he had locked her in. She would fake surprise when he told her, thank him politely for the keys, then in her most businesslike way, show him the door. And that should be the end of Mr. Duffy.

Three cups of coffee later she was checking her watch against the kitchen clock wondering what in hell was keeping him. How dare he make her sit and wait? She wanted to get her running in before the temperature rose too high. If she dropped from heat exhaustion when she ran it would be entirely his fault.

At eight thirty her patience was at an end. She called down to Chloe, hoping she would pick her lock once again so she could leave an apartment that seemed to be fast closing in on her. She had some misgivings, as she was sure Chloe would still be sleeping, but instead the phone wasn't answered at all.

At eight forty-five, her rage building, she was pacing the apartment, ready to kill the first person who came in the door. Retribution for such treatment was foremost in her mind.

At nine she snatched her computer chess set off the shelf and plugged it in, then sat down at the table for a calming game. If anything could take her mind off her predicament, it would be chess. She moved the queen's pawn and set the game in motion.

Three moves later she heard the key in the lock

and tensed. She concentrated on the game, not even looking at the door, and moments later was aware of Duffy standing by the table looking down at her.

"I knew it. I knew you wouldn't panic. Anyone else would have broken a window and screamed for help, but not you."

She made her move, totally ignoring his presence.

"Know how I knew that? You're not the type. There are certain psychological types who panic in a given situation, but I could tell you weren't one of those when I saw how coolly you reacted to your apartment being broken into. No, not you—you'd be too embarrassed for anyone to know you got yourself into this kind of situation to begin with."

He walked into the kitchen and she could hear him put more water on to boil. She felt like telling him to forget it, that he wasn't staying long enough for coffee, but she didn't feel like giving him the satisfaction of speaking at all.

"You might even get your picture in the New York *Post*. And you sure wouldn't like that, would you? Not quite the proper image for a rising young executive, am I right? Might even hit the front page. I can just see it—you peering out from behind your windowgate—another of their one-day wonders."

Caroline noted the pattern of bars the sunlight was throwing across the room and suddenly felt as though she were jailed and his talking was the psychological torture devised just for her. Much more of it and she felt she'd scream. And the fact that he read her so correctly didn't go down well, either.

"Like a cup?" he asked, as though speaking to an old friend.

She finally looked up at him, her face impassive and then caught her breath. He was dressed in a red T-shirt and tight, in fact very tight, jeans. She caught a glimpse of his chest hair peeking out of the V of his shirt, then looked further up to see laughing blue eyes and dark curls tumbling over his forehead. She had forgotten how very good-looking he was. Even his mouth was sexy on the few occasions when it wasn't moving. She felt her body responding to him even while her mind was telling her to get rid of him as quickly as possible.

He fixed two cups of coffee and brought them over to the table, then set down a plate of jelly donuts beside the chess set.

"I thought maybe you would have worked up an appetite by the time I got here. Sorry about curtailing your running this morning, but we did get in a little exercise last night, am I right? Not too talkative this morning, are you? That's too bad—I'm pretty cheerful in the morning, always enjoy having some conversation at the breakfast table. Oh well, we're compatible in other ways."

Caroline watched as he bit into a donut, the outside covered with sugar and the inside literally oozing with delicious looking jelly.

His obnoxious cheerful voice, the smell of the

jelly donut and now the sounds of smacking lips all converged to unnerve her momentarily, and she made a stupid move, the kind she might have gotten away with with a human opponent, but the computer never seemed to make a mistake. The computer's light started flashing instantly, almost in glee, and she realized at once that her fatal move had all but ended the game.

"Bad move," said Duffy, reaching for his second jelly donut. "You really ought to try one of these—they're still warm. Or don't you eat stuff like this? You into health food along with all that exercise?"

Caroline eyed the donut warily, then quickly looked back at the board. Junk food happened to be her nemesis. Just wave a pizza under her nose and she was off. Visions of fast food filled her head when she jogged: hamburgers from McDonald's, greasy southern fried chicken, banana splits piled high with whipped cream and chopped nuts, Twinkies, candy bars... the list was endless. At the moment jelly donuts headed the list. She tried to concentrate on the game, knowing she couldn't eat before running and working out, but fast losing her desire to do either.

No sooner had she made her move than the entire board lit up, flashing on and off in an infuriating manner. This happened whenever the computer beat her, which was most of the time. Conversely, when she beat the computer the board merely went dead. No lights. She never

even got the satisfaction of seeing them all flash
for her victory. She switched it off and got up
from the table.

Which was another bad move. He now had a
clear view of her long, bare legs in the running
shorts and her braless form beneath the top. His
eyes were assessing her body with the kind of concentration she should have given to the chess
game. She quickly sat down again, folding her arms
in front of her to partially block his view. The man
continued to unnerve her. He was biting into his
third donut now and the only thing worse than
watching him eat was hearing his incessant chatter
when he wasn't eating. She was certain he didn't
really want a third donut, that he was eating this
one simply to annoy her further. All in all, his behavior was really very childish.

"Mr. Duffy," she said coolly, "I have heard of
children having temper tantrums when they don't
get their own way. I have also observed that men
are basically children. In my opinion, however,
locking me in was carrying a tantrum to a dangerous extreme. You could go to jail for your actions,
you know."

Duffy merely looked pleased that she was finally
speaking to him. "First of all, Caroline, I was not
having a temper tantrum. And how would you describe your behavior? Refusing to speak to me, not
even eating a jelly donut—that's adult, I suppose.
As for my going to jail—is that a threat? I don't
believe it for a minute. You wouldn't let yourself in

for that kind of publicity—it might shatter your dignity."

Caroline felt like taking the rest of the jelly doughnuts and shoving them in his supercilious face. "What if there had been a fire?" she asked him, her voice betraying her anger.

She felt a sense of satisfaction at the look of worry that crossed his face. "I hadn't thought of that," he admitted. "Not that the fire department couldn't have broken down your door," he added.

"You mean my pick-proof door?" she asked sweetly.

"It's wood—they could have used a hatchet on it."

"For your information," Caroline informed him, "Chloe picked that pick-proof lock in about thirty seconds. With a hairpin!"

His eyebrows rose in incredulity. "*Chloe* did?"

She nodded.

He gave her a sheepish grin and spread his arms. "Well, I defy your average burglar to."

"You mean Chloe's better than the average burglar?"

"Sure. I taught her. Comes in handy for a super to know."

Caroline noticed her hand snaking toward the plate of donuts and quickly stopped it. "All I want to know, Duffy, all I really want to know is why you did it. Why did you lock me in?"

"Why do you think I did it?"

"I assume it had something to do with my one-time-only policy. I figured that got to your ego and you decided to lock me in and take me a second time by force."

"You thought I'd rape you?"

"It crossed my mind."

"I wouldn't do anything like that!"

"If you'd lock me in..."

"No, that's different. I swear to God, I wouldn't force you."

"You forced me to stay in my apartment."

"That's different—that didn't hurt you."

"It could have. You did a stupid, criminal thing, and I think I'm entitled to know why you did it. You studied psychology, you ought to be able to come up with an answer."

She lit a cigarette and watched as he ran his hands through his curly hair, leaving traces of powdered sugar in their wake. He seemed a little nervous now, even remorseful. He had even given up on the jelly donuts.

"I guess you think I'm a nut," he said at last.

"I don't think it was a rational act." She certainly wasn't going to start feeling sorry for him now. Who was the victim, anyway?

"Since when is love rational?"

"What?"

He was nodding his head now, not meeting her eyes. "I couldn't believe it when I came to your door last night and saw that it was you. I mean, I used to *wish* you'd get robbed."

"Thanks a lot."

"How else was I going to meet you? I tried saying good morning to you a couple of times, but you just ignored me as you ran by."

Not only was he the neighborhood shrink, but now he appeared also to be the neighborhood romantic. "You wouldn't believe how many men say things to you when you run in this city, and they're usually not as innocuous as 'good morning.'"

"As it was, it's a miracle you called my place for a lock."

"Miracle? I could wallpaper the entire apartment with the fliers I received from you."

"I kept sending them to your whole building because I didn't know which apartment you lived in."

Caroline couldn't remember ever having had anyone fall in love with her at first sight before. "I find it hard to believe my looks just struck you dead, Duffy."

"I like the way you look. But if you had turned out to be like most of the women I meet, I wouldn't have been interested even though I think you're great looking. But you're different. I've never met anyone like you."

"There are lots of women like me."

"Maybe, but I don't know any."

"That still doesn't explain why you locked me up."

He started to say something, then stopped, then shrugged. "You said you didn't want to see me again."

"I always thought I had free will."

Out of sheer nervousness, it seemed, Duffy was now biting into his fourth donut and not endearing himself to her at all. "I feel foolish trying to explain it to you."

"I felt foolish being locked up," she countered, not letting him off the hook.

"I just figured...I don't know...I thought if I could just get you captive for a while..."

"Yes?" she prompted him.

"I thought I could get you to fall in love with me."

Caroline laughed. "Love by coercion? That's an interesting theory."

"No, you can't force someone to love you. Listen, we were hitting it off last night, weren't we?"

"Briefly."

"I'm not talking about the sex. Well, not just about the sex. I enjoy talking to you."

He enjoyed talking period, she felt like saying. "Why do you want me to fall in love with you?"

"Unrequited love's not really my thing."

"Any kind of love isn't my thing," said Caroline.

"You're not normal."

"That's my problem!"

"Well, it's my problem now; I'm in love with you."

"How can you be in love with me, Duffy? You don't even know me."

"How can I get to know you if I don't see you?"

"It's really only a physical attraction anyway," she said, thinking of her conversation with Chloe.

"Oh, it's that all right, but it's also more. And I also know it isn't one-sided, it's just that you're too damn stubborn to admit it."

"Oh, I admit there's a physical attraction, but I'm certainly not in love with you."

He smiled. "I think we're just using different words, that's all. Look, I know I've gone about this backwards. Usually we'd get to know each other and then, eventually, go to bed. But in our case... anyway, why can't we get to know each other now? Do you want to go to a movie tonight?"

"I don't go to movies; I have Home Box Office."

"That's no good, it's not like a real movie where you eat popcorn and hold hands."

"I like it better."

"I don't know about you, Caroline. You use a calculator because you don't trust real arithmetic, you watch Home Box Office instead of going to the movies, you play chess against a computer... you don't seem to want to live in the real world."

"Those things *are* the real world. I think you're living in the past. Aren't you a little young for nostalgia, Duffy?"

"It's not nostalgia. I just appreciate real things. Hell, you even have a moose head instead of a pet!"

"If you'd just listen to yourself you'd see we

have nothing in common." *Except jelly donuts,* she thought, unable to resist any longer. One couldn't hurt her, she reasoned, taking a bite of the still-warm donut.

Duffy didn't even seem to notice she was eating. "Why do things have to change? Did you ever watch old movies on TV when you were a kid? God, I really loved Westerns. The men were always out on their horses shooting it up, being heroes. And then they'd go home to their women who'd be fixing dinner in the cabin. The women always wore bonnets and had curly hair and everyone knew where they belonged. Did you ever see those movies?"

"Sure," said Caroline, swallowing the last of the donut. "I always wanted to be Billy the Kid."

Duffy gave her an annoyed look. "You never pictured yourself in the kitchen wearing a bonnet?"

"Listen, Duffy, if you had a choice of picturing yourself out riding a horse and having a good time or always standing around a hot stove, which would you choose?"

"But I'm a man!"

"Well, I think women are just as adventurous as men. Maybe more so, but the men were always bigger so they didn't allow us to be. What about those old war movies, Duffy? I bet you liked those, too. Do you really think that when we watched those movies we pictured ourselves as the sweethearts left behind? Hell no! Each and every one of us was down in that submarine saying 'up periscope' at the crucial moment.''

He leaned across the table and took her hand. "I understand what you're saying; I really do. I don't blame women for what they want—intellectually I understand it perfectly. But it's really messed things up for everyone and I can't help wishing it never happened. I mean, if you're going to be logical about it, we couldn't both be out riding horses all day, who'd keep the cabin clean and take care of the kids and do the cooking?''

Caroline freed her hand in order to partake of another jelly donut. She could always go to the gym later in the day when she'd had time to digest the food. "If we were both free we could both be out riding horses all day. I'm serious, Duffy—I don't want love, I want adventures.''

"You could have your adventures with me.''

She chuckled. "Your idea of adventure is probably hitting the flea markets on Saturdays and picking up antique locks.'' She saw a gleam in his eyes. "Hit home with that one, didn't I? I bet you're really settled down in that house of yours on Staten Island. All you probably need to make it complete is a housewife to keep it clean. Preferably one wearing a bonnet.''

"I could change.''

"No, you couldn't. You'd probably want to cage your wife in that house of yours on that godforsaken island just like you caged me up here. Throw her a few jelly donuts to keep her happy. I know why you're attracted to me, Duffy—it's because I'm independent, and independence in a woman really gnaws at you. You feel like you just have to do something about it. I came to the conclusion a long time ago that the world is made up of two kinds of people—those who want to be free and those who want to take that freedom away. And I guess a lot of people like me just finally get worn down by people like you and eventually give in. And a lot of that wearing down is done in the name of love, only what most people mean by love is a desire to possess. And I'm not going to be someone's possession, Duffy, not ever!" She paused in amazement at herself. "Sorry, I didn't intend making a speech."

"Don't apologize; I was impressed."

She got up from the table and took their two cups out to the kitchen. "You want some more coffee?"

"Love some. If it's any satisfaction to you, Caroline, I was awake all night worrying about locking you in. I don't know what came over me; I swear I've never done anything that outrageous before."

"I had no trouble sleeping," she told him.

"You know something? You never react like a woman."

"I just don't conform to your conception of how a woman should react, that's all."

"I mean it. A normal woman would have either found it romantic to be locked up by her lover or else would have been frightened to death. You just went to sleep. You know something? I don't think you picture yourself as a woman."

"That's ridiculous."

"I don't think so. It's like what we were just talking about, you always pictured yourself as the hero of the movies. What about *Robin Hood*, did you ever see that movie?"

"Six times."

"Who were you, Robin Hood or Maid Marian?"

"Robin Hood."

"And pirate movies, what about them?"

"I wanted to be the pirate. But so what? That doesn't mean I see myself as a man. I just always preferred action to inaction, and the men always got the parts with the action. It's like my job. I don't want to be a man in the business world. I want to be a woman outmaneuvering the men."

"You're pretty competitive, aren't you?"

"Is that bad?"

"I don't know. Maybe not if you just confine it to your work. Hell, I guess I should be thankful you are the way you are, otherwise you might have called the police on me."

"I still might. I'm really a law-abiding person, Duffy; I don't think crime should pay."

"This hasn't exactly paid."

Caroline set the coffee down on the table and resumed her seat. "If you had it to do over, would you still lock me in?"

He grimaced. "I'd think twice about it!"

Caroline felt unaccountably annoyed at his answer. The very first time a man had made such a romantic gesture toward her and already he was regretting it. "I thought briefly of knocking you over the head when you came back and then tying you up," she told him.

He eyed her over his fifth jelly donut. "What stopped you?"

She reached for another donut before they all disappeared from the plate. "I didn't see any point in it. Keeping you here when I don't really want you here would be rather self-defeating."

"So that's it, then? You're really not going to see me again?"

"I told you how I am, Duffy."

"I still think that's a fouled-up system of yours. One time only..."

"A system is only fouled-up if it doesn't work. Mine works." Which was easy enough to say since it was the first time she had tried it.

"How do you know a two-time-only policy wouldn't work just as well?"

"I just have a feeling it wouldn't."

"What makes you think so?"

She shrugged. "Today's a good example. I like you better than last night. See? That's the problem, I'm getting to know you."

She was surprised to realize that she meant it. She was beginning to like him better. There was something enjoyable about sitting across the table from him, eating jelly donuts and arguing.

He smiled at her. "I think that's terrific!"

She shook her head. "No, it isn't. I have no intention of getting involved, so what's the point of
getting to know you? And if I get to know you, I
might get to like you, in fact I already like you and I
don't even know you very well, and I'm not going
to get involved even if I get to know you and get to
like you, so what's the point of getting to know you
in the first place?" She saw he was looking confused. "Did you understand that?"

"Could you say it again more slowly?"

"I don't think so."

"Listen, Caroline. I just don't think you should
exclude the possibility of a relationship from your
life. There are all kinds of relationships these days —
all kinds of marriages. It wouldn't have to be like a
prison. and I'm not talking about a relationship
with me, I just mean in general."

Caroline stared at him for a long moment,
tempted to pursue the conversation further. "I'll
keep that in mind, Duffy, but the truth of the matter is, this would be the very worst point of my
career to get involved with a man. I just don't have
the time."

She saw several conflicting emotions cross his
face, then he leaned back in his chair with a sigh.
"All right, Caroline, I give up. But I like you too
much just to let it go at that. Couldn't we be
friends?"

She had to admit she thought he was giving up a
little precipitously. If she were in his place she
wouldn't give up so easily. But that was the differ-

ence between them—she was the adventurous one while he was already settled down in a house. "What does being friends include?" she asked.

He raised his hands in a gesture of mock surrender. "No sex, you have my word. It would just be fun to get together once in a while, talk, maybe have a game of chess. You said you ate out most of the time and I hate cooking just for myself. Maybe we could have dinner together once in a while— dutch, of course."

It did get lonely eating by herself all the·time, she admitted to herself. Why not? It wouldn't hurt to be friends with Duffy; it would probably even be fun. She might eventually even get him to run with her in the mornings.

"Okay, Duffy—I'd like to be friends."

He smiled and held his hand out to her, and she put her sugar-covered one in his. "A deal, then— friends."

"Friends," she repeated.

"How about having dinner together tonight?"

"Duffy!"

"Why not? You have anything better to do? Just dinner, and then we'll go our separate ways."

No reasonable excuse came to mind, so she finally nodded in acquiescence. "All right, just dinner."

"You ever been to Chinatown?"

She shook her head.

"You like Chinese food?"

"Love it."

He stood up. "Great, I'll pick you up at seven."

She stood up and walked him to the door. "You don't need to pick me up, I'll meet you at your shop. After all, we're friends, right?"

He smiled. "Right. See you then." He was out of the door and she was closing it when he suddenly turned and came inside again.

With a laugh, he reached into his pocket and took out a ring of keys. "Almost locked you in again, it must be becoming a habit," he joked, handing her the keys. Then, without any warning, he leaned down and kissed her on the nose.

"Don't take it personally," he said, his eyes dancing. "There was a spot of sugar there I couldn't resist."

He was gone then and the apartment suddenly seemed very empty and quiet without him. She had known him...what? Not even twenty-four hours, and yet in some way the apartment had become partly his. No, it wasn't quite that, she reasoned with herself, it was probably just the windowgates that reminded her of him. And the new lock on the door. And the two empty coffee cups on the table. And, of course, the rest of those insidious jelly donuts, which she would throw away immediately and not even think about eating!

Her nose felt warm where he had kissed it. A nose with feelings? She didn't believe it. She'd have to watch that. Her body was giving her signals that had nothing whatsoever to do with friendship. But her nose?

She threw the jelly donuts out before she could change her mind, then put the dirty cups in the sink and ran water into them. She got her purse, picked up her laundry bag, then tried to open the door without unlocking it first. Which was going to take some getting used to, having to open it from the inside with a key.

It was another hot, humid day and she was already sweating by the time she reached the laundry on Third Avenue. She left her things with the attendant to be washed and dried, then headed over to Second Avenue and up to Thirty-fourth Street to her health club. She spent an hour lifting weights and working out on the Nautilus equipment. She was proud of the muscles she was developing, proud of the strength she was attaining. She knew Duffy would give her an argument about that too. He would probably say it was just one more indication of how she thought of herself as a man, not a woman, but she knew he was wrong. It was just his old-fashioned, outdated notions about women. She didn't see anything unfeminine about muscles in a woman. It felt good to push her body to its limits, build up her endurance. Her body looked better and felt better now than it had when she was eighteen.

She took a shower, wrapped herself in a towel and went into the sauna. The dry heat lulled her into a half-sleep and she consciously tried to clear her mind of all thoughts and just totally relax. It proved to be an impossibility. Thoughts of Duffy kept invading her mind, fragments of their arguments, the way his dark hair fell over his forehead, the moments when his blue eyes darkened and almost looked black. When she found herself reenacting in her mind how they had made love, she knew she was going too far. That was no way to be thinking about a friend!

After the sauna she was tempted to swim for an hour instead of running. It was a hot day and the water would feel so good. But she had chosen running as her form of aerobic exercise and decided she better stick to it. Like everything else in her well-scheduled life, running had its place, and to change things on the spur of the moment would lead to sloppy thinking. And planning. And eventually to a sloppy life.

Leaving the gym she headed up Second Avenue at a run. The sidewalks were crowded with people doing their Saturday shopping, walking dogs, just walking aimlessly, and a few other runners. When she got to Forty-eighth Street she slowed down and then stopped in front of a store window, pretending to look at the display. Instead she lit a cigarette, hoping no one around would notice that she had stopped running in order to smoke.

In the books she had read on running they had all said smokers who ran would find themselves giving smoking up after a while. She had hoped it would be true, but no such thing seemed to be happening to her. She smoked the cigarette furtively, as though it were something other than a legally sold Benson & Hedges Light. Nobody was even looking at her, but she still felt somehow guilty.

When she had smoked it halfway down, she put it out and continued her run. Even with the smoking her breath control was good; she practically never got winded anymore.

She ran up to Fifty-ninth Street, then turned west to Third Avenue and headed back downtown. At Thirty-third Street she went into McDonald's for a hamburger and Coke. It was hard to rationalize having more junk food after the jelly donuts of that morning, but the healthy Chinese food she was to have for dinner should make up for the lapse.

Back in the lobby of her building she ran into Chloe who was dragging in a shopping cart full of groceries.

"Hey, how did it go with Duffy?" she was asked.

"Great. We've decided to be friends," Caroline told her, then related briefly what had happened that morning.

But Chloe looked disbelieving. "You can't be friends with Duffy—I don't believe it!"

"Why not? Don't you think he's capable of being friends with a woman?"

"Sure, *I'm* friends with him, it's not that. It's the two of you! Fated lovers, the two people more perfect for each other than any I've ever met, and you're going to be *friends*? That's criminal!"

Caroline was still laughing when she got off the

elevator at her floor. Star-crossed lovers indeed! Criminal? On the contrary. It would probably prevent Duffy from doing anything criminal again. She was sure he'd never try locking up another woman, not if it meant they ended up just friends.

Chapter Six

Caroline walked into Duffy's shop at seven. It was far larger than she had supposed from the outside. Behind the long counter the wall held an array of locks, but the other two walls were hung with different types of wrought-iron grillwork painted in a variety of colors. It was more like a showroom than a typical locksmith shop where one would go to get a key made.

"If that's you, Caroline, I'm back here," called Duffy, and she walked through the door that led to the back. Duffy was sitting in an office partioned off from the rest of the room which held the equipment to manufacture the grillwork she had just looked over. He was seated at a desk going over some papers and smiled at her when she took the chair next to his desk.

"This is quite impressive," Caroline admitted to him. "You make your own grills?"

He nodded. "I have three men employed full-time putting them together. There's a big demand for security in this city. Just give me another minute and we can leave," he said, looking back down at the papers.

He must keep clothes at the shop, she was thinking as her eyes traveled over him. He was dressed impeccably in white pants, a beige silk shirt and a navy blue blazer. He looked freshly shaved and his hair still looked damp. He looked quite as impressive as the rich oilmen she had come into contact with in Texas and not at all like the original Duffy she had met in his working clothes.

She was dressed in a white cotton skirt made of tiers of ruffles and a white camisole top edged with antique lace. Her hair was held back from her face with two combs and she had fastened pearl earrings in her lobes. She had decided on a skirt and top more because of the heat than to show him she could dress just as femininely as the next woman, although that had occurred to her. Now she was glad. It was obvious they were going to a nice restaurant and she wouldn't have liked embarrassing him by wearing her old jeans and running shoes.

He handed her several sheets of paper with a smile. "You're the financial expert, want to take a look at these for me?"

A brief glance told her it was a bid on a job, quite a sizable one from the looks of it. The bid was on a security system for a new forty floor office building and her eyes automatically went to the figures at the right as her hand reached into her purse for her pocket calculator. She heard his laugh and looked up.

"I do use a calculator in my work," he said.

"Then why do you want me to look at it?"

"I never had finance in school; I just wondered if the overall bid looked right to you."

She glanced down at it again. "It seems to be in order. That's a nice profit you'll be making if you get the job."

"You have to take into consideration the fact that I'll have to hire several men to work full-time on it. That money doesn't all go to me."

"Still...I guess I didn't think your business was so extensive."

He laughed. "You thought I just installed locks on doors?"

Caroline, who had thought exactly that, shrugged. "I guess I didn't think about it at all."

He switched off the lamp on his desk and stood up. "Come on, let's go—I'm starved. Haven't eaten since those donuts this morning."

She followed him out of the shop and watched as he pulled an iron gate across the front of the building and fastened it with a strong padlock. Then he led her down the street to where he had parked his van and held the door for her while she climbed inside.

He started the motor and turned on the air conditioner, letting the interior cool off before pulling off down the street.

"Is that effect calculated?" he asked, glancing down at her.

"What effect?"

"The virginal, pure look. You've somehow managed to look like a sweet, old-fashioned girl."

Caroline contained the laugh that was bubbling up inside of her. It wasn't that she didn't trust Duffy to stick to their new friendship, but she hadn't thought the "untouchable" look could hurt. The last thing she would have worn would have been something even remotely sexy. "How do you know I'm not a sweet, old-fashioned girl," she asked him in a teasing voice.

He turned right on Second Avenue and headed downtown. "Now that's a subject I think we'd better avoid," he told her. "Unless, of course, you feel like discussing some of our more prurient activities of last night."

Caroline thought better of her teasing and changed the subject. "I'm excited about going to Chinatown," she told him. "I haven't had any good Chinese food since I left California."

"You like Szechuan?" he asked her.

"I don't even know what it is."

"Chinese, but very hot. Maybe too hot for you, but we could get one dish and let you try it."

"I'm a Californian, remember? I was brought up on hot Mexican food. I think I can take it."

They were still discussing food, both of them having a healthy interest in it, when she noticed that he was turning into a line of cars and saw the water just ahead of them.

"Where are we?" she asked, looking out the window for the first time in a while.

"That's the Staten Island Ferry just ahead of us."

"The *what*? I didn't know Chinatown was on Staten Island."

"It isn't."

She looked at him with growing suspicion. "Then why are we here?"

"I decided to take you to my house for dinner instead."

So much for ever trusting men, thought Caroline, giving him an angry look. "How *dare* you assume I'd want to go to your house for dinner!"

"I'm a good cook." He didn't seem in the least ruffled, which infuriated her even further.

"I don't care *what* kind of cook you are, I have no intention of eating at your house. Now turn right around and head for Chinatown or this friendship is ended as of now!"

He gave a low chuckle and the van began to move. At first she thought he was doing as she said, but then she realized they were pulling onto the ferry.

"All right, that's it, Duffy," she said in a tightly controlled voice as she reached for the door handle and pulled it down. Nothing happened.

She looked to see if the lock was down, but there wasn't the usual lock on the door. She tried pushing harder but nothing happened. "All right—how do I get out of here?"

"You don't."

"Listen, Duffy, I've had enough of your games. Let me out of this van this instant."

"I'm afraid you're not going anywhere, Caroline. Except to Staten Island, that is."

She went to roll down the window, but there was no handle. They were now on the ferry and wedged in so tightly by the other cars he couldn't have turned around if he had wanted to. She tried the door handle again, but it still didn't open.

"Forget it, Caroline, I fixed the door this afternoon so you wouldn't be able to get out."

She turned to him in fury, so angry she was shaking. "This is kidnapping, do you know that? This is even worse than locking me in my apartment!" she practically shouted.

He gave an amused chuckle. "It is, isn't it? Well, once a criminal..."

She could pound on the window, scream for help, cause such a scene that maybe she'd attract some attention. She would also feel very foolish trying to explain to someone why she was all dressed up and apparently out on a date and that her date just happened to fix the lock on the door and was taking her to Staten Island against her will. It was like a scene out of a very bad movie, one she wouldn't have believed for a moment.

"Is this your idea of friendship?" she asked him sarcastically.

Again there was the answering chuckle. "We were never friends, Caroline."

"But you said—"

"I lied."

"This is even more despicable than locking me up!"

"Desperate situations take desperate measures."

That rotten man had the nerve to sound pleased with himself! She opened her purse and took out her cigarettes. She could at least make him feel very uncomfortable by filling up his van with smoke, polluting his air space.

She inhaled the cigarette but it didn't have its usual calming effect. "Forget it, Duffy—I've seen the movie and it isn't going to work."

"What movie is that?" he asked, rolling down his window a couple of inches to let out the smoke.

"The one where the psycho kidnapped the girl and kept her in a cage in his basement. Like you, I think he had some mistaken notion she would fall in love with him in the end."

"And did she?"

"No—she died."

He laughed out loud. "Don't get so dramatic, Caroline; you're not going to die. I'm just inviting you to spend a pleasant weekend with me, that's all."

"And I'm refusing the invitation!"

"I'm afraid it's too late for that."

"I have no intention of spending the rest of what has already been a disastrous weekend in some desolate house on your barren island. You might get me there, but the only way you'll keep me there is by tying me up, and you're going to have a hard time of it if you try to do that."

"First of all, Caroline, I don't know where you've gotten your views of Staten Island, but it's part of New York City, you know. It's hardly barren and my house is anything but desolate. As for tying you up, I really doubt whether that will be necessary."

"That's what you think," she muttered, reaching to put her cigarette out in the ashtray.

"By the way, Chloe stopped by to see me today. Gave me hell, you'll be glad to hear, but she also told me something very interesting."

Caroline stared out the window at the top of the car next to them and ignored him.

"Did you know we were perfectly matched? According to the stars, anyway."

"I should have known you'd believe in that nonsense."

"I can't say that I ever did before, but she showed me our charts and it was really incredible how complementary they were."

"The only way we're perfectly matched is in our criminal intents. You felt like kidnapping me and I feel like murdering you!"

"It was fate—destined—don't try to fight it."

She gave a sigh of exasperation. She had been warned about the criminal element in New York; she just hadn't been warned what guise it would come in. On the surface he would seem intelligent, educated, urbane. While all the time, lurking underneath, was some crazy romantic! She should have stuck to football players; at least Billy's game plan had been easy to comprehend.

"I thought you'd find it romantic. Like one of those old pirate movies where the beautiful maiden was kidnapped by the pirate chief and carried off to his ship."

"To be ravished."

"No, the movies in those days didn't go that far."

"Anyway, I told you. I would have been the pirate, not the one being kidnapped."

"Then you can kidnap me."

"I don't want to kidnap you!"

He reached over and smoothed back a tendril of her hair that had slipped out of the comb. She overreacted, slapping away his hand as though he had been attacking her, and in the next moment he had moved along the seat until he was next to her and she was practically shoved flat against the door.

"Don't touch me, Duffy!"

"How can I ravish you if I don't touch you?" he asked softly, and before she could answer he had turned to her, his body half covering hers, and then his mouth was pressed hard against hers and no matter how hard she tried she couldn't move it away from him.

She tried to kick him and one of his legs moved over hers, effectively pinning her to the seat. All that running, all that weight lifting, and she still seemed to be powerless against a larger male. It just wasn't fair, she was thinking, when one of his hands slipped down the front of her camisole top and closed over her bare breast. She felt herself shudder at the touch. She decided to totally relax, put him off his guard, and then, when he also was relaxed, she would make her move.

Her mouth parted beneath his and when his tongue sought entrance she didn't demur, her own arms going around his strong back and pulling him closer. That's right, come into my trap, she was thinking, but then his other hand was sliding up her leg beneath her skirt until it finally settled on the soft skin of her inner thigh. What she had thought of as a trap was instead an entrapment. Her body's natural responses were taking over, her thighs now imprisoning his hand, her hardened nipple pressing against his other hand, her own tongue entering his warm mouth and exploring its depths. She could no longer understand why she had even wanted to trap him; this was what she wanted, only this, his hard body crushing her, his skillful hands exploring her curves, his mouth merging with hers until they were breathing the same air. The force of her passion was literally jarring her, and then he was lifting himself off her and she realized the jarring was external, not internal. The ferry was docking and for the last few minutes she hadn't even been aware of where she was.

"Sorry," he murmured, moving over again behind the wheel. "I generally like to finish what I start, but in this case..."

She looked out the window with horror. Anyone could have seen what they had been doing and she hadn't even cared. She hadn't even thought of it.

"Don't worry," he said, reading her thoughts, "the van's too high up for anyone in cars to have been able to see us."

Still trembling with desire, she lit a cigarette with shaky fingers. She couldn't even yell at him, re-monstrate—she had been putty in his hands, quite willing to let him do as he wished. Quite willing, in fact, to even help him along. She suddenly hated herself for her lack of control, her loss of dignity. What was happening to her that she could allow this man, this man she hated at the moment, to reduce her to this?

He was driving onto the dock now and put one arm across the back of the seat. "Come over and sit next to me, love," he said, his voice a soft caress.

It was all she could do to stop herself from mov-ing over and snuggling up against him, wanting to feel his strong arm enfold her. She wanted to rest her head on his chest, slip her hand inside his shirt and run it along his chest. She wanted...she wanted him to make love to her, and the thought was so disheartening she felt like crying.

He reached over and put one hand on her thigh and she felt an electric current run through her. And then she was brought down to earth with a thud when she heard the self-satisfied tone in his voice when he said, "You still want to get out of the van?"

She knocked his hand off her leg and turned to him, her eyes narrowed, her voice deadly. "You're damn right I do!"

He seemed startled by her swift, unexpected reaction. So he thought he had her eating out of his hand by now, did he? He had a lot to learn if he thought she was that easily subued.

"If I believed that for a minute, I'd stop the van right now and let you out."

"Try it," she taunted him.

"Caroline, Caroline," he said, as though speaking to a child, a not very bright child at that. "You might think you know what you want, but your body tells me differently. Why don't you just resign yourself to the fact that the stars don't lie. We were meant for each other, and the sooner you accept that fact the easier it will be for you."

Caroline folded her arms across her chest and stared out the window in stony silence. Her body was telling her differently too, but so far in her life she had been ruled by her mind, and she was quite certain that momentary lapse would not occur again. Next time he made a move on her she would quite effectively put him out of action for at least the duration of this weekend, and she'd make damn sure he never got another chance. At least they had taught her something in that self-defense course she had taken.

"I can see those wheels in your mind going into

gear right now," he was chuckling. "I can't wait to
see what you have in mind for me."

If you knew, you'd be able to wait, she thought
wryly.

"Methinks the lady doth protest too much, isn't
that how it goes?" He was laughing now, amusing
himself no end.

She couldn't wait to see that smirk wiped right
off his silly face! She had never met up with a more
monumental ego. Once, when she had been maybe
eighteen or nineteen, she had the secret notion
that she could get any boy to like her if she could
only get him to ask her out for just one date. By
twenty-one she had found it just didn't work that
way; some men were attracted to her, others
weren't, and no amount of wishful thinking on her
part could change that. Duffy didn't seem to have
gotten past the wishful thinking stage. Lock her up
and she'd fall in love with him. Kidnap her and
she'd fall at his feet with desire. What utter nonsense!

They were driving in silence, Duffy, it seemed, having finally exhausted his repertoire of repartee. She
watched out of the window as they passed apartment complexes, small shopping centers, then
drove through a more sparsely settled area with occasional old houses. Just when she was envisioning
Duffy living like a hermit in the middle of no-
where, they turned a corner into a development of
new houses, most of them two-storied, set in a

semicircle facing away from the road. He parked the van in a communal carpark at the end of the houses, got out of the van, then went around to open the door on her side.

She got down from the van in silence and let him lead her around the carpark to where the houses faced the water. Leading to the water was an Olympic-size swimming pool with an area surrounding it containing grass and picnic tables and gas barbecues. At the end she could see two tennis courts in use. There were several young couples around, some swimming, some relaxing in deck chairs, and one heading in their direction.

Just as Caroline was trying to decide whether to ask help from the couple, perhaps a ride to the ferry, the slim blonde in the bikini gave Duffy a hug and said, "Good, you're just in time. The coals are all ready and we were just about to put on the steaks."

She turned to Caroline and held out her hand. "I'm Pat, and the walrus here is John."

He did look like a walrus with his hair slicked back by the water, his drooping mustache and his sleek, wet body, and she almost laughed as she took his outstretched hand.

"You can laugh," John told her, "just tell me how you like your steak first."

"Rare," she told him, "and my name is Caroline."

"Welcome, Caroline," said Pat. "You have time for a quick swim, if you like."

"I forgot to tell her to bring a suit," said Duffy, putting a friendly arm across her shoulders.

Caroline didn't mention that telling her to bring a bathing suit to a Chinese restaurant would have been a bit suspect. The couple seemed nice and a steak would be welcome; it was not the time or the place to start a scene, Caroline decided.

"You can borrow one of mine," Pat was offering, but Duffy interupted, saying he needed her to help him with the salad.

Not wanting to appear rude in front of his friends by refusing to help with the dinner, Caroline followed Duffy as he headed for one of the houses. It was a split-level, very modern, of redwood and stone and lots of large windows overlooking the water. He unlocked the front door and led her inside, then down some steps to a kitchen in the back.

What she could see of the house seemed to be done in earth tones—browns and grays and some touches of moss green, altogether different from what she had been expecting. For some reason she had him pictured living in some old, maybe Victorian, house filled with bric-a-brac and antiques.

The kitchen had butcher-block counters and cupboards, white appliances, gleaming copper pans hanging from the ceiling, and was totally immaculate. She stood in the doorway and watched as Duffy took lettuce, tomatoes, cucumbers, and an onion out of the refrigerator and placed them on one of the counters. Then he took a knife down from one of the racks and handed it to her. "You can either murder me now or start the salad while I change my clothes," he told her with a grin.

She debated the options for a moment, then silently took the knife and moved over to the counter. Eating took priority for the moment, she decided.

She had found a large plastic bowl in one of the cupboards and had the salad all prepared when she turned to see that he had appeared and was leaning against the doorway in a navy blue bathing suit that fit what it covered like a glove. She figured he must keep in shape by swimming a lot.

"No need to stare, you've got all night to enjoy my body," he told her in his usual infuriating manner, opening the door to the refrigerator and taking out a jar. "My speciality—best salad dressing you've ever tasted."

Not having anything pleasant to say in reply, Caroline again kept silent. She would be nice to his friends, enjoy her dinner, but after that...watch out, Duffy!

Two other couples were already seated at the picnic table when Caroline and Duffy sat down and he introduced her all around. Over steaks, hot German potato salad, Duffy's salad, and later ice-cream sundaes, Caroline got to know the couples. All of them worked in the city, women as well as men, and they were all in agreement that Staten Island was the place to live.

Pat and John were both Wall Street lawyers and

after John finished telling her what an easy commute it was, Pat confided that they had been robbed three times before they decided to move.

Caroline related her own robbery of the day before, and when Pat asked, "Then you've only known Duffy since yesterday?" it took a moment to answer.

Caroline laughed. "I guess it was only yesterday, but it seems much longer." At the moment she could hardly remember *not* knowing Duffy.

"It was in the stars, though," said Duffy, then told them about their charts. After that there was a lively debate regarding astrology, Caroline siding with the majority who considered it nonsense.

Caroline, feeling overdressed among the bathing-suit clad crowd, took up Pat's offer to borrow a suit, and after coffee she followed Pat into her house to change.

The red bikini was a little loose on her, but she tied it tightly and considered herself lucky it wasn't too small instead. She wanted to swim, but she didn't want to appear to be enticing Duffy in any way. Not that he seemed to need enticement.

Pat showed her around the house before they returned to the pool. It was all done in green and white with shaggy green carpeting throughout, lots of white wicker furniture, and plants everywhere. Caroline thought it was charming and told her so.

"We love it here," confided Pat. "For the same amount of money all we'd be able to get in the city would be a one bedroom. Here we have all this

Harlequin reaches into the hearts and minds of women across America to bring you

Harlequin American Romance.™

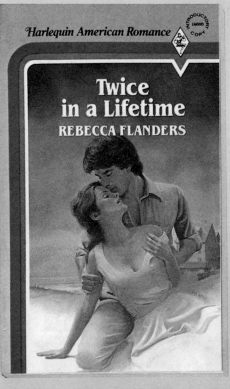

Harlequin American Romance

INTRODUCTORY COPY 16000

Twice in a Lifetime
REBECCA FLANDERS

YOURS FREE!

Enter a uniquely American world of romance with *Harlequin American Romance.*™

Harlequin American Romances are the first romances to explore today's new love relationships. These compelling romance novels reach into the hearts and minds of women across America...probing into the most intimate moments of romance, love and desire.

You'll follow romantic heroines and irresistible men as they boldy face confusing choices. Career first, love later? Love without marriage? Long-distance relationships? All the experiences that make love real are captured in the tender, loving pages of *Harlequin American Romance*.

What makes American women so different when it comes to love? Find out with *Harlequin American Romance!*

Send for your introductory FREE book now.

GET THIS BOOK FREE!

Harlequin American Romance

Twice in a Lifetime
REBECCA FLANDERS

room plus the pool and tennis courts. And the neighbors are great—we all have lots of parties. Sundays we have our famous brunch around the pool—I hope you'll be here."

"I'm sure I'll be here," said Caroline with a wry smile.

"Great! Duffy's really terrific, isn't he?"

"Well, he's certainly full of surprises," said Caroline.

"You don't know how many friends I've introduced to him, hoping something would come of it. But he's so damn particular, it's really infuriating. He always says he'll know the right woman when she comes along, and then there'll be no stopping him... Oh, sorry, I probably shouldn't be babbling like this to you."

"Don't worry about it," laughed Caroline. "Anyway, I'm not the right woman."

"I'm sorry to hear that, because it sure looks like Duffy thinks you are. I've never seen him look at a woman the way he looks at you."

Caroline shrugged. "Maybe he thinks I am, but he's wrong. As far as I'm concerned men aren't part of my plans at the moment; I'm too busy right now with my career."

"Oh, men don't have to interfere with your career unless you let them. I think if you find the right man you should go for it—things have a way of working out, but the right man might not come along twice."

Caroline, who wasn't keen on the conversation,

changed the subject and they both headed out to
the pool. A net had been strung across the pool and
a volleyball game was in progress. Caroline and Pat
jumped in the water on the women's side and got
into the game. Caroline found herself laughing and
enjoying the game as much as the others, and even
felt pleased whenever Duffy complimented her on
a good return. She couldn't remember having had
such a good time in months, maybe not even then.
It had really been as long ago as college since
she had gotten together with friends and had fun
like this. And it had been that long since she had
had any close women friends, something Caroline
found she missed. She wished things had been different and she had met Pat in the city. It wasn't
likely she'd be able to be friends with any of
Duffy's friends, not when she never planned on
seeing him again.

When the volleyball game broke up, Caroline
swam several lengths then noticed Duffy sitting on
the side of the pool watching her. She swam over
to him and grabbed on to the ledge. "I like your
friends," she said.

"They're good people."

"How did you happen to buy a house here, anyway?"

"I did the locks and the security for the development and decided I liked the place. I was looking to
invest in some real estate, anyway, and I decided it
might as well be in something I'd enjoy."

She half expected him to make some sort of grab

at her even with other people around, but instead he seemed content to just sit there and relax. "You're different here," she observed, speaking her thought out loud.

"Different? How?"

She had noticed it at dinner. While with her he seemed to be argumentative, always talking, always making some smart remark that would make her angry, with his friends he had intelligent discussions and they all seemed to like and respect him. "I don't know," she finally said. "Easier to get along with, I guess."

"I'm usually easy to get along with."

"Then why do you always manage to make me so furious?"

He chuckled. "Oh, I do that on purpose; I love to see you get mad."

"What would your friends say if they knew what you did to me?"

He raised a brow and gave her a mocking smile. "What did I do to you, Caroline?"

"You know what I'm talking about. What would they think if I told them you locked me up overnight and then kidnapped me to bring me here?"

"Why don't you ask them?"

Caroline realized this wasn't something she could do at this point. After all, she was hardly acting like a prisoner. "I can't very well ask them," she said.

"Then I guess you'll never know."

"Hey, folks, we're having a poker game if you want to join," John shouted over to him.

"You interested?" Duffy asked her.

She was already pulling herself out of the pool. "Sure, I'm interested," she told him, heading toward the picnic table where three other couples were seated. Anything to prolong the moment when she'd have to be alone with him, she told herself. And it would also be a distinct pleasure to beat him royally at poker.

Chapter Seven

"You've got to learn how to bluff," he told her as he opened the front door to his house. It was shortly after one and the poker game had just broken up.

"I *know* how to bluff," she said angrily.

"Then how come I called your bluff every time?"

"Because you stayed in every damn game, that's why! And staying in every game, whether you have anything or not, is really poor poker playing!"

"Then why is it I won and you lost?"

He was leaning back against the door, smiling down at her, and she wished nothing more at the moment than to be able to wipe that superior grin right off his face. "Because you were lucky, that's why. It doesn't take any skill to stay in every game."

"Even when you win?"

"You play poker like a child—just like you do everything."

His smile became wider. *"Everything?"*

"Don't bring sex into the conversation!"

"But you said 'everything.'" He pushed a switch and some lamps went on in the living room. She walked into the room, looking around.

Caroline was tired and would have liked to mention bed, but was afraid he'd get the wrong idea. She knew he'd get the wrong idea. She'd also like a shower; her hair felt sticky from the chlorine in the water. The living room was dominated by a large, stone fireplace, surrounded by low, comfortable looking furniture. Two couches faced each other, each big enough to sleep on comfortably if he didn't have a guest room. She didn't imagine he did have one; probably his guests were all female and all eager to share his bed.

There was a wet bar in one corner, the requisite stereo system and color TV, even a low table and four chairs to be used for cards or eating or whatever...

"Would it be all right if I took a shower?" she asked, feeling the leaves of a large tree she could have sworn was fake but turned out to be real to the touch.

"Sure—use the bathroom off the master bedroom."

She looked around, but saw no doors leading off the living room. "Where is it?"

He pointed down the hallway and when she passed him in the direction he was pointing, he was still leaning against the door, rather like he thought

he was single-handedly holding up the house.
Well, he could move fast when he wanted to. Nota-
bly in the van on the ferry, but also, as she recalled, in the volleyball game. His lazy demeanor
was sometimes deceptive.

She turned into the first room she came to and
was reasonably certain when she had turned on the
light that it was indeed the master bedroom. What
struck her first was the fireplace, a working one by
the looks of it. She had always thought the height
of luxury would be to have a fireplace in the bedroom.

A voice behind her said, "Do you want me to
light it?"

She swung around. "Are you crazy? In this
heat?" she replied, although it was considerably
cooler out here than it was in the city.

"I can put the air conditioner on along with it."

"There happens to be an energy crisis, or weren't
you aware of it?"

He chuckled. "You're in the oil industry, tell me
about it."

She was not about to be lured into another argument. He'd probably turn out to be anti-oil, and
that could really develop into a fight. She glanced
briefly at the very large platform bed covered with
some kind of furry spread, then headed toward
what looked like the bathroom door. It was.

She turned on the light and stared at the luxurious bathroom. The tub was large and square
and sunken, surrounded by very beautiful tiles in

an Egyptian looking pattern. There were double sinks in the long, marble-topped counter, antique wall sconces that gave the room a soft light, and one corner held an ornate bamboo chair surrounded by potted palms. If she had a bathroom like that, she was sure she would spend wasteful hours in it.

She closed the door to the bedroom and locked it. Not that it would probably hold against his use of a credit card, but somehow she didn't think he'd break in on her in the bathroom. She stripped off her clothes, then pulled the transparent shower curtain around the tub before stepping inside. She turned on the water to lukewarm, then soaped her body and let the water rinse out her hair. When she got out, she wrapped her hair in one of the towels and put on the white terry-cloth robe she found hanging behind the door. She wore her panties under the robe, but left the camisole and skirt hanging behind the door.

Only one lamp was lit when she entered the bedroom. Most of the light came from the logs that were burning in the fireplace. It was warm, but not too warm; she noted that the air conditioner was also on.

In front of the fireplace were two wing chairs with a small table set between. A bottle of wine and two glasses were now on the table along with a chess set ready for a game. He was sitting in one of the chairs watching her reaction.

"That's really a terrible waste," she had to say.

"One night isn't going to affect the energy crisis," he said. "And you must admit it's romantic."

He was dressed in brown pajamas, silk by the looks of them, and she had to admit it made a romantic picture. The only thing spoiling it was her with her hair up in a towel. She stood there, feeling a little ill at ease. It had now turned into an old Cary Grant movie only she didn't look right for the part. She also, she reminded herself, wasn't in the mood for the part.

"Where do I sleep?" she finally asked.

"I thought we'd have a game first," he said, pouring the wine into the glasses and motioning for her to sit in the other chair.

Not wanting to appear churlish, she took the proffered chair and picked up the glass of wine.

He reached out and touched his glass to hers. "To us," he said, his look guileless.

"Duffy!"

He shrugged. "All right—to the moment."

She took a drink of the wine and looked down at the board. He had set it up so that she was white, so she moved her king's pawn.

His eyes were still on her. "Shall we make a wager to make it more interesting?"

It mattered little to her since she was confident she would beat him. If he played chess as childishly as he played poker, there would be no contest. "If you like."

He chuckled. "Am I right in assuming you're determined to fight off any attempts on my part to make love tonight? Even though that's exactly what you want?"

She ignored the last part. "You're correct."

"Then let's say if I win, your one-time-only policy changes to a two-time-only policy."

She shrugged indifferently. "And if *I* win?"

"Whatever you want. I'll drive you home tonight, if that's what you want. Or I'll sleep on the couch. It's up to you."

She shook her head. "That's not equitable. You'll be winning something if you win, but if I win I'll merely be getting out of something."

"Then you name it."

"If I win I want you to never bother me again. A day ago you didn't exist for me; I'd like it to go back to that."

He smiled. "Not even friends?"

"You've already pulled that one once, Duffy."

"Is that really what you want?"

She nodded, wishing desperately for a cigarette. She had smoked her last ones during the poker game and now she felt in need of one.

"All right, then."

"Listen, is there anywhere around here I could get some cigarettes?"

He laughed. "Oh, is that why you were looking so nervous?" He got up and went over to a chest of drawers. When he returned, he handed her an unopened pack of cigarettes and a lighter.

"I thought you didn't smoke," she said, getting the pack open and lighting a cigarette.

"I used to. I keep a pack around to remind myself I'm strong enough to do without them."

"How did you do it?"

"I just decided one day to see how long I could go without one."

"How long has it been?"

"About a year."

"Does it bother you that I smoke?"

"If you mean does it make me want to light up, no. If you mean does it bother me to see you killing yourself, yes."

"Go to hell," she muttered.

He laughed. "That's better, now you're back to your old self. I didn't recognize us being so polite there for a while."

He made his move and she began to concentrate on the game. It was immediately apparent that he played chess well, well enough that he could beat her if she wasn't very careful. It was extremely important to her that she not lose the game to him. It had nothing whatsoever to do with the sex. Sitting across from him in the softly lit room and feeling the warmth of the crackling fire, the view of the bed large and inviting over his shoulder, Duffy looking handsome and sexy with the silk of his pajamas playing over the muscles beneath, she knew she wanted him. The physical attraction was as strong as ever—maybe stronger. What's more, she had liked him very much over the last few hours. No, she wanted to make love with him, but she wanted it to be on her terms, not his.

She didn't want to go to bed with him because he had won that right in a game. She wanted to win, then go to him freely, of her own accord. She didn't want to see his mocking smile as he placed her king in check or hear that all too familiar chuckle when he claimed his bounty. She didn't want coercion to enter into it at all, and that would only be possible if she were the victor and he the vanquished. And, of course, she also liked to win.

She lighted another cigarette and filled her glass with more wine. He was maddeningly slow in his moves, much slower than the computer, and it was getting on her nerves. Because of this, she made her moves too quickly, her way of telling him her mind worked more quickly than his, but he hardly seemed to notice. Either he was half asleep or his concentration was greater than hers. She chose to think it was the wine and the heat of the fire that was lulling him.

He shifted his legs beneath the table, the silk of his pajamas brushing against her bare leg where the robe had come apart. She felt an involuntary shudder run through her and she pulled the robe more closely around her.

His eyes immediately fastened on hers. "You're not cold, are you? You want me to turn the air conditioner down?"

She shook her head. "No, I'm fine. Just make your move."

But he wasn't to be hurried. He reached out and put one hand over hers and his eyes moved back to the board. His fingers moved slowly, tracing the contours of her hand, the touch absorbing all her attention so that when he did move, her well thought out strategy seemed to fly from her mind and she made a move only a fool would have made. She immediately saw her mistake but tried to stay calm, hoping he wouldn't notice it. The computer would have noticed it, of course, but maybe his attention had wandered as hers seemed to be doing and he wouldn't notice.

His hand tightened over hers and she looked into dark blue eyes that held a familiar gleam. "If I didn't know you better, Caroline, I would think you're deliberately trying to throw the game in order to get into bed with me."

She snatched her hand out of his grasp. "That would be the last thing I'd do," she almost hissed. Damn the man for noticing and then calling her move into question in such a despicable way.

"This game I can win without your help. You might say I'm highly motivated."

"No more so than I am," she told him quickly.

"I don't mind your lying to me, Caroline, but why don't you quit lying to yourself? If you didn't want to go to bed with me you wouldn't still be here."

"What choice did I have?" she asked, the tenuous hold on her temper disintegrating.

"You had many choices. I'm sure Pat or John would have been happy to drive you to the ferry. Or one of the others."

"I didn't want to embarrass you in front of your friends," she said.

"Do you really believe that? If you had really wanted to leave, would you have let my embarrassment stop you? How far would you go to maintain your dignity, Caroline? If a rapist attacked you on the street would you decline to scream for fear of embarrassment?"

"That's a rotten thing to say!"

"Think about it. Do you only use those overly good manners of yours when it suits you to do so?"

"At least I have manners!"

He spread out his arms in a supplicating gesture. "Am I being ungentlemanly in any way? You're sitting in my room, wearing my robe, drinking my wine, smoking my cigarettes, having just availed yourself of my shower...what more do you want of me, Caroline? Have I been remiss in any way?" As though no thought had gone into it at all, he negligently made his move.

Stung by the truthfulness of his words, Caroline moved her queen, and too late saw the trap she had walked into.

"Check," he said with a smile. A real smile, not supercilious or leering or amused, but one that expressed his pure pleasure of the moment.

She sat there stupefied that he could have rattled her enough to make her lose the game so easily. Maybe it was her own fault for having played with a computer for so long. She was unused to human opponents who talked and prodded and teased, unnerving her to the point where she couldn't have even played a good game of checkers.

She stood up and undid the tie on the robe, letting it fall away from her body and exposing her breasts to his view. "You win, let's go to bed," she said, a defeated look on her face.

"Put the robe back on," he commanded her, "and sit down. If you think it's going to be quick, unfeeling sex like last night, you're mistaken."

"I'd rather just get it over with," she said sullenly.

"I'm sure you would, but I'm the winner and we're going to do it my way this time." He stood up and pulled her robe together, tying it again in front and then putting his hands on her shoulders and exerting pressure until she was once again seated in the chair.

He offered her a cigarette, lit it for her, then poured them each some more wine. As she sat smoking, he went into the bathroom, returning with a hairbrush. Removing the towel from her head, he stood behind her and began to brush her hair dry.

"If this is supposed to get me in the mood..." she muttered.

"No. It's supposed to get *me* in the mood. I don't happen to find wet heads appealing in bed."

At first she found the rhythmic brushing relaxing, and she leaned back in the chair, letting her hair fall over the back toward the fire. Soon, though, the feel of the brush through her hair began to feel sensuous and the tingling of her scalp was echoed by a tingling sensation throughout her body.

"Does that feel good?" asked Duffy.

"It feels all right." Testily.

"You just can't help censoring your feelings, can you? Couldn't you just once say what you really feel?"

"It feels...relaxing."

"Relaxing and what else?"

"I don't know...tingling, I guess. But maybe that's the wine."

"And maybe it's the fact that you're alone with me in my bedroom."

"I doubt that."

"Caroline!"

"All right. I suppose that has something to do with it," she conceded.

"Are you looking forward to making love with me?"

She was silent for a moment. "If you ever get around to it."

"Oh, you needn't fear about that."

"It's getting late."

"We have all night, darling."

"Spare me the endearments."

He paused in his brushing. "You know what I really ought to do with this hairbrush, don't you?"

"What's stopping you? It would fit right in with your macho image, wouldn't it?"

"Don't tempt me, Caroline." The brushing resumed, but the arguing hadn't had the desired effect; she still wanted him. More by the moment.

When he finally put the brush down and ran his fingers through her hair, it was dry and felt like a swath of silk on her neck. He walked around the chair and stood in front of her, then reached out for her hands.

She let him lift her to her feet, then stood motionless as his arms went around her and his head bent to kiss her. He did nothing at first but hold her close and kiss her slowly, gently, his mouth imperceptibly moving back and forth across her own. When his tongue began to trace the outline of her lips, she found that her hands had somehow found their way to his hair and she was running her fingers through the springy curls, then pulling his head harder against her so that their mouths were suddenly kissing with more intensity. Her lips parted and his hard tongue began to probe the depths as her tongue dueled with his. She lifted herself on her toes, moving closer to him, wanting to feel his body against her. When one hand moved to unbutton his pajama top so that she could feel his bare chest pressed against her, he took her hand and moved it away, pausing in his kissing long enough to murmur, "Don't be in such a hurry, darling."

She found she couldn't help being in such a hurry. Her body felt on fire and she knew that fire would not be quenched until she gave vent to the desires she was feeling, feeding the flames until they exploded in ecstasy. She had never thought of herself as particularly passionate, but all Duffy seemed to have to do was touch her to set her off. She pressed herself against him, willing him to take her, but his kissing went on and on. When he finally stopped, after what seemed like an eternity, he held her away from him and looked down into her bewildered brown eyes.

"I know. I feel the same," he told her. "No one else has ever affected me in quite this way."

She was surprised to feel exultant at his words, but didn't have time to think about it as he was taking her hand and leading her over to the bed.

At last, she thought, as he undid her robe and pulled it over her arms, letting it drop to the floor. His warm hands reached inside her panties, sliding them down over her hips and legs to end up in a small pile on the floor. Then, without first removing his pajamas, he lifted her off the floor and set her gently in the center of the bed.

"Don't rush me, I want to make love to every inch of you," he said softly, burying his face in her neck and finding her pulse. He kissed her there gently as one hand trailed lazily down the side of her body, setting off reactions wherever it touched. When she tried to reach for him, he took both of her wrists in one large hand, effectively pinning them. "Don't fight me, Caroline. Just relax, my love."

He kissed her throat, her shoulders, the top of her chest, then moved down where his mouth captured one taut nipple. As she felt it being sucked into his mouth, her body arched against him, wanting to be free to wrap itself around him. He kept her pinned to the bed as his mouth sent charges from her breast all through her body, and his other hand rubbed back and forth against her remaining breast. She had always thought foreplay was an unnecessary prelude to love, but his mastery of her responses was overwhelming her to the point where she realized there was more to lovemaking than she had ever supposed.

Her body was being bombarded with sensations as his hand and mouth worked her to a feverish pitch. Even his chest hair rubbing against her stomach was exciting her, even the way one strong leg lay trapped between her own.

His mouth moved off her breast, traveled to the other, then, when she thought she could bear it no longer, began its slow descent down her body, stopping, teasing, tantalizing her with his tongue, then moving on. She shuddered as it moved close to the core of her sexuality, but this was bypassed as his mouth moved to between her thighs, then kissed the length of her legs. One toe went between his teeth to be nipped on playfully, and even this she found erotic, her body one mass of indistinguishable sensations at this point. She was no longer thinking of hurrying it up and finishing it; all she was thinking was that she never wanted it to stop.

His head moved back up and he was doing

things to her she had never allowed a man to do before, thinking them too intimate, not wanting to share that much of herself. And yet there was no question that it felt right, that it was what she wanted. Her body was lifting to meet his tongue, her moans and cries inarticulate as she felt herself being lifted to heights never before attainable. She felt herself peaking, and then splintering into a million fragile pieces, pieces that he then carefully fit back together to once more take her on that long ride. She felt exhausted, drained, and then in the next moment capable of anything.

She slowly became aware that he had stopped. She opened her eyes to see him quickly shedding his pajamas, then straddling her waiting body. She reached for him, her eyes filled with a desperate yearning, mirroring the feelings she was no longer trying to hide.

He smiled at her while his eyes remained serious. "I love you too," he murmured, then lowered himself until they were joined. He made love to her slowly, tenderly, kissing her all the while. She couldn't begin to give a name to her feelings; she just knew that they felt as one and that it felt right. He wasn't playing gymnastics in bed; instead he was loving her in the most intimate way possible, and she appreciated the difference.

They rode the waves together and when they mounted the crest, they reached the top at the same moment in time, clinging to each other at the force of the explosion. It was only then that their mouths parted, each gasping for air as their bodies slowly shuddered to a standstill.

He rolled to his side, taking her with him and holding her close. He didn't speak, just held her tight, his strong arms reassuring her still shaken body. Exhausted, content, at peace, she fell asleep.

She awakened to find herself covered by a sheet, with Duffy, propped up on one elbow, gazing down at her.

"Good morning," he said, his hand reaching out to brush the hair out of her eyes.

"Good morning," she said, smiling at him in return. She stretched, then curled up facing him.

"It's almost noon. Am I to assume you're not a morning person?"

"No, I'm usually up early. It must have been late—"

He was nodding. "Yes, it was. Good, we're both morning people. How do you want your eggs?"

"Just coffee will be fine."

"Nonsense. You've got to keep up your strength. The weekend isn't over yet, you know."

She reached for him but he moved out of her way. "That wasn't an invitation, Caroline. At the moment I'm starved. For food," he added.

"I hope we don't have to play chess every time," she teased.

He got out of bed and put on his pajama bottoms. "Patience, Caroline. Now how do you want your eggs?"

She gave him a mischievous look. "I like my eggs scrambled, my coffee black, and I thought men liked sex in the morning."

He was laughing as he left the room. "The morning's not over yet," he called to her from down the hall.

Caroline took a quick shower, used his toothbrush, and was back in bed wearing one of his T-shirts she had found in a drawer when he returned with the breakfast tray and the Sunday *Times*. Behind him trailed a multicolored cat who leaped onto the bed, stared suspiciously at Caroline for a moment, then turned around in circles a couple of times before settling down on her ankles.

"Is that your cat?" she asked, quickly drinking some of the coffee. It was good, much better than the instant she made.

"Yeah, that's Clyde."

"I didn't see him last night."

"I never had the heart to have him fixed, so he isn't around much of the time. He comes home occasionally to fill up on food and rest."

She reached for some buttered toast and the business section of the paper.

"Is that what you always read first?" he asked her.

"Ummm."

"What do you read next?"

"The front section and then the travel."

"You're unnatural," he said.

"I am not unnatural—those are what interest

me. And I don't read cookbooks or fashion magazines, either." She reached for some of the scrambled eggs he was quickly demolishing.

"Good, we have that in common too. I don't read cookbooks or fashion magazines, either."

"I'm relieved to hear that," she told him and he laughed.

Caroline's foot was going to sleep from the weight of the cat and she tried to gently pull it out from under him. The cat retaliated by biting her hard on the ankle. "Your cat just bit me, Duffy."

"He's protecting his territory."

"You *sleep* with him?"

"He sleeps with me."

"Then why doesn't he sleep on your legs?"

"Because I'd kick him off the bed."

She tried to kick Clyde off the bed, but he bit her again and she decided to concede the fight. Anyway, it was kind of nice, being in bed with Duffy, having breakfast, reading the paper companionably. It would be even nicer, of course, if the cat liked her. She pushed the paper aside and reached out to pet the cat behind the ears, something she had heard cats liked. Clyde obviously hadn't heard that piece of cat folklore because he wrapped his large paws around her wrist and bit her hand. She turned to see Duffy convulsed in laughter.

"Is that cat like that with everyone?" she asked indignantly.

"You make it sound as though I've had scores of people in this bed with me."

"Not people. Women."

"Do I detect a trace of jealousy, Caroline?"

"No, you do not. I'm just wondering why your cat dislikes me so much."

"You've got to show him who's master."

"I thought that was with a horse."

"It works with Clyde too."

Caroline eyed the cat warily and decided not to try to show him who was the master. Clearly the master was the one with the sharper teeth and claws.

Later, when the breakfast was eaten and the paper read, Duffy reached for the cat and dumped him unceremoniously over the side of the bed. He was just reaching for Caroline when the cat leaped back up, placing himself between them this time. Duffy reached for a section of the paper and slapped Clyde across the rump. The cat hissed but didn't move.

With a deep sigh, Duffy got out of bed and headed toward the kitchen. At the first sound of something rattling, the cat leaped off the bed and raced out the door. Duffy quickly came in and closed the door behind him.

"How'd you accomplish that?" Caroline asked him.

"Rattled some cat food."

"That's showing him who's master." She laughed.

"Never mind Clyde," he said, his mouth effectively silencing any reply she might have made.

Chapter Eight

"Weren't we supposed to have brunch with your neighbors?" Caroline asked him, her head resting on his furry chest.

"Did you want to?"

"No."

"Neither did I." His arm tightened around her.

She was trying to decide whether she wanted a cigarette enough to leave the warmth of his arms to get it. Her bad habit won out, but he didn't seem to mind when she returned to bed and placed an ashtray on his stomach.

"Do you mind my smoking in bed?" she asked.

"Not at all—you're a guest. When you move in with me, however, I expect you to give up that filthy habit."

"Then I expect I'll be smoking a good long time," she said flippantly, smiling at him.

"Don't you like my house?"

"I love it—it's great."

"You could change it if you wanted."

"It's perfect the way it is. I'm impressed, actually. I had expected something quite different."

His foot began rubbing against her ankle. She wasn't sure whether he was nervous or whether he was feeling amorous again, but couldn't wait to find out.

"What did you expect?"

"Oh, some kind of old, Gothic place filled with antiques. A wife in a bonnet wouldn't exactly fit your decor."

"You liked my friends, didn't you?"

"Very much. I'd love to get to know them better."

"And the sex? Any complaints?"

"You searching for compliments, Duffy? I wouldn't have thought there was anything wrong with your ego in that department."

He chuckled. "All right, so we're in agreement about that. And while we're on the subject of sex, can you honestly say that you still think one-night stands are better than two-night stands?"

She had an urge to tell him the truth, but something still held her back. "Brief encounters, Duffy, not one-night stands."

"Whatever."

"Well, I must admit the second night was better."

"Did you enjoy the volleyball game?"

"Yes."

"The poker, the chess—"

"Don't push your luck!"

"Can't stand to lose, can you?"

"I won't lose the next time."

"Admit it, Caroline—we're perfect for each other."

She thought back to the night before, to something as ordinary as the dinner table conversation. She and Duffy and the others had discussed everything from politics and the economy to astrology and the World Series race. She thought about how seldom she'd ever talked to Billy about anything beyond their own limited interests: his football, her work. Everything had been so shallow, so limited, the only common denominator being sex. She wondered what it would be like to live with someone who could work up a rhetorical sweat on any number of subjects. And she realized something else: It had been quite some time since she'd found him overtalkative and annoying. One of them must've mellowed, or else it was a blending of them both.

"You might be the right person, Duffy, but it's still the wrong time."

"Oh, I don't know—I'm ready to settle down."

"I'm not."

He took her cigarette out of her hand and stubbed it out in the ashtray. "You still think marriage is some kind of cage? Those couples you met last night, the wives all have their own careers, hell, the husbands wouldn't have it any other way. You'd still be free, Caroline."

"You really believe that?"

"Hell, yes!"

"All right, supposing we were married, Duffy, and I got transferred to Saudi Arabia? What would happen then?"

"What if I dropped dead? You can think of a million ifs, but most of them aren't likely to happen in the near future."

"It's very possible I could be transferred to the Mideast. That's where we're doing most of our business, you know."

"You wouldn't have to accept the transfer."

"I'd want to. It would be a promotion, what I've been working toward."

He moved away from her, running his fingers through his hair. "From what I've heard, those Arabs don't like doing business with a woman."

She had heard that too. "Which would make it quite a challenge. Don't you think I'd like to prove myself to be the exception? So what would you do? Come with me and let me support you?"

His face looked grim. "If that was the only way we could be together."

"You're lying—you're not the type to let a wife support you."

He gave a wry smile. "I could always set myself up in business over there, be a camel trader or something."

"I think they're mostly driving Cadillacs these days."

"That's even better. I know a lot more about

cars than I do about camels. I could install locks on gas tanks.''

"Gas is probably free there—who would steal it?'' She reached over and touched his face, bristly and rather boyish looking at the moment. "You know you wouldn't do it, Duffy.''

He was silent for a long moment. "You're right; I wouldn't.'' He got out of bed and headed for the bathroom. "However, I don't think that's anything we have to worry about now. We'll face the problem when we come to it, and just maybe we'll never come to it.'' The bathroom door shut and she heard the sound of the shower being turned on.

She reached for the magazine section of the paper and thumbed through it as her mind wandered, her thoughts on Duffy and the weekend they had spent, mostly in each other's company. It was a comfortable feeling being in his house, reading the Sunday paper in his bed, talking to him over breakfast. She found him easy to talk to, fun to argue with, and of course she truly enjoyed the sex. He did seem to be well suited to her, much better suited, in fact, than any of the other men she had known.

She felt it was too soon to make any definite commitment. Duffy might run his life on impulses, but she didn't. The best thing to do would be to wait and see whether their relationship strengthened or weakened over a period of time. If it strengthened, fine; then she would give it some serious consideration. If, on the other hand, it weakened, then they'd both be glad they hadn't rushed into anything rashly.

She'd have to make it clear to Duffy, though, that those childish shenanigans of his—locking her in, kidnapping her—would have to stop. He would just have to learn how to carry on an adult relationship, one where each respected the other's freedom.

It would be nice to have someone to do things with in New York. She was tired of always eating alone, going to the theater alone, taking long, lonely walks. It was a city of couples, she saw them everywhere. Having Sunday brunch in sidewalk cafés, attending concerts in Central Park, standing in line for the movies, the people were always in twos, but now she'd be with Duffy. Weeknights he could occasionally spend at her apartment. It would be convenient for him, working just across the street. Weekends they could go to his house, maybe entertain his neighbors or just sit around and relax.

And that's enough planning in advance, she told herself. Don't treat it like a business problem— leave some margin for the unexpected. With a chuckle, she reached for the sports section of the paper. She was looking to see how the Dodgers did when Duffy came into the bedroom, a towel wrapped around his waist.

"How about a swim?" he asked.

"Ohmigod," she muttered, a small item having caught her eye.

"Well, we don't have to swim. Too bad you didn't bring tennis clothes."

"Billy's been traded to the Jets," she said, scanning the item again for confirmation.

"You mean Billy Tyler? Yeah, I saw that. You a Jet fan?"

"No, I'm a Ram fan."

"Lousy team," he said cheerfully, "and they're not going to get any better this year."

"You support your home team, don't you? Well, so do I."

"Yeah, but my home team wins."

"Give me a break, Duffy—the Rams have consistently won more seasons than the Jets ever will." Her mind wasn't on her words, though, it was on Billy coming to New York. He'd be sure to look her up, probably think they'd continue where they left off.

"Why the interest in Tyler?" he was asking her, and when he repeated it the words penetrated.

"I used to go with him," she said casually, setting aside the newspaper and stretching.

"One of your one-night stands?" asked Duffy, his eyebrows providing the sarcasm.

"I said I *went* with him. Going with someone is hardly a one-night stand."

"Yeah, but you told me—"

"I lied."

He stopped in the middle of putting on his bathing trunks and looked at her. "What do you mean you lied?"

She shrugged. "I lied, that's all. Actually, you were my first one-night stand, although I guess you could say you weren't even one."

He was standing stock-still, his trunks in his hand, his eyes narrowed. "Are you telling me that the whole scenario you went through the other night was all lies?"

She chuckled. "I thought you'd be glad to hear it."

"What else have you lied about?" His eyes were darkening now and she stopped smiling.

Caroline suddenly felt ridiculous arguing with him naked, and pulled the sheet up to cover her body. She couldn't understand what he was getting so angry about, but for once she was determined to keep her own temper under control. "What's the big deal? Would you prefer I had only one-night stands and scheduled my sex twice a month?"

His voice was icy. "I'd prefer a little honesty."

She was kneeling on the bed now, the sheet clutched around her. "Well, I really doubt that, Duffy. I told you exactly what you wanted to hear!"

"What I wanted to hear was the truth!"

Getting angry now, and not wanting to conduct her side of the fight from the position of the bed, Caroline got up and stalked into the bathroom, slamming the door behind her. She quickly got into her clothes and emerged a few moments later. "No, you didn't want to hear the truth, Duffy. You wouldn't have even believed the truth. You had me pegged as some hard-nosed businesswoman who called all the shots, remember? Asked men out for dates? Made the first move? Do you happen to remember that, Duffy, or has it conveniently slipped your mind?''

"So this whole thing has just been a charade with you, is that it?'' He had his trunks on now and his look was menacing. Caroline stayed on her side of the room.

"I didn't even know you when I told you those things, Duffy. You were a stranger—an extremely nosy stranger.''

"It seems to me you'd already been to bed with that 'extremely nosy stranger' when you gave your little spiel about fortnightly sex.''

"Yes, and now I'm regretting it!'' She reached for the cigarettes and drew the last one out of the pack. Damn him for upsetting things just when she thought they were getting along so well.

He was leaning against the wall now, his thumbs hooked into the waistband of his trunks. "You're not the only one who's regretting it.'' His voice held no emotion at all.

"Good. Then maybe we ought to just call it quits right now.'' She was damned if she was going to let him get those words in first.

"Not just yet, Caroline. I want to hear about Billy Tyler. Just how long did you 'go' with him?''

"I don't think that's any of your business.''

"I'm just curious, that's all. A week? Two weeks? A month?''

"A year and a half."

There was a long silence. "I see. And when did it end?"

"A few weeks ago. When I was transferred here."

He walked over to one of the chairs and sat down. His fingers began drumming out rhythms on the arms and she could actually see the tenseness in his shoulders. "So tell me, Caroline, was it a tearful farewell? Do you keep in touch?"

"No to both questions," she answered tersely.

"No? Well, what did happen?"

"Nothing happened. I told him I was being transferred, he asked me to marry him, and that was that. I really don't care to discuss it any further."

"Whoa! He asked you to marry him?"

"That's right."

"And you refused?"

"Of course."

"Surely after a year and a half you must have come to feel something for him."

"Of course I did." Caroline stubbed out her cigarette, desperately wishing that there were more.

"And yet you refused?"

"I was being transferred, Duffy. It was a promotion. What kind of marriage could survive with one partner living in Houston and the other in New York?"

"So you just walked away, with no regrets?"

"That's right."

"You are one coldhearted bitch, Caroline, you know that?"

"We parted friends."

"You parted friends...I see. So when *your* transfer came, *your* job promotion, you just walked away and that was that. *Finis!*"

"I wasn't ready for marriage."

"Are you ever going to be ready?"

"I doubt it!" She spat out the words.

He was nodding his head now, his fingers still drumming. "So that's what I'd have to look forward to with you, is that it? Some transfer would come through, and good-bye Duffy."

She stared at him, wondering how they had gotten to this icy coldness between them when only a short while before...

"I asked you a question, Caroline."

"And you answered it." Her words had a finality to them that surprised her. They also had the sound of an excellent exit line, and she thought she better take advantage of it before things became even stickier. She grabbed up her purse and headed out of the room.

"Caroline!" His voice was a command.

"See you around, Duffy," she said, heading for the front door.

The glare of the sunshine and the heat came as a shock after the cool interior of the house. Caroline stood a moment shivering as the sun began to warm her body and her eyes adjusted to the light.

"Caroline, over here!" She looked toward the pool and saw Pat waving to her.

Pat was just getting out of the pool as Caroline

walked up. "Could I ask a huge favor of you, Pat?"

"If you want to use my suit again, help yourself. John's playing tennis so you'll have the house to yourself."

"No, it's not that," she said, hating to have to tell Pat the truth. "I was wondering if you could drive me to the ferry. I hate to ask . . ."

Pat glanced toward Duffy's house. "You two having problems?"

Caroline gave her a wry smile. "You could call it that."

"Why don't you have a swim? Maybe things will cool down and look different to you."

"Nothing's going to look different, I'm afraid."

Pat gave a decisive nod. "Okay, hang on a minute while I get my keys."

Duffy hadn't appeared by the time they got in Pat's car and drove off, which was a relief to Caroline. She would have hated for him to cause a scene in front of his friends, but felt he was quite capable of doing it.

"Want to talk about it?" Pat asked after a while.

"Things just didn't work out. Duffy is a very stubborn, argumentative man."

"Aren't they all," drawled Pat with a chuckle.

"I really appreciate the ride, Pat. I had envisioned a long, hot walk."

"Don't mention it. I'm just sorry things turned out the way they did. I was rooting for the two of you. Hoping to get to know you better."

"We could always get together for lunch."

Pat's expression brightened. "Yes, let's. If you look in the glove compartment you'll find one of my cards. Give me a call anytime, and if I'm not in court..."

Caroline had thought she'd enjoy the ride back to Manhattan on the ferry. This time she would be free, not locked up in his van, but she found the ride hot and boring. She was glad to get a taxi right away in front of the terminal building and gave the driver her address. She looked at her wrist and found that she had left her watch on Duffy's bedside table. She only hoped he wouldn't find it necessary to return it to her. Probably not. He'd probably just mail it to her if he did anything at all. She didn't think he was any more eager to see her again than she was to see him.

The taxi stopped in front of her apartment building and Caroline got out. Chloe was in front of the building watering the few scraggly bushes with a hose.

"Where have you been? I've been trying to talk to you all day," Chloe called out, then turned off the hose as Caroline approached her.

"Don't tell me my apartment's been broken into again," said Caroline, but Chloe shook her head.

"No, nothing like that. I just wanted to warn you that according to your horoscope you better stay away from Duffy today. If you see him, something dire is sure to happen."

Caroline gave her a rueful look. "It already has."

"You mean you've already been with him?"

She nodded.

"I saw you two drive off together last night, but I figured he brought you home. Does this mean the 'friendship' didn't work out?"

Caroline's body seemed to slump. "Oh, Chloe, I don't know how to explain it. It went from friendship to something more and right now we're not even speaking. It's all over and not even worth talking about."

Chloe shoved the hose back behind the bushes and opened the door to the building. "Come on inside, have a cup of tea and tell me all about it."

"It'll bore you to death, Chloe."

"Are you kidding? This is better than a soap opera."

Not feeling strong enough to protest, Caroline followed her in the building. She took a seat at Chloe's table and didn't even demur when the cup of green tea was placed in front of her. She briefly related the events of the last eighteen hours, then said, "You can see why I had to walk out, can't you?"

"Of course. I can also see why Duffy lost his temper."

"Big deal, so I lied to him. He kidnapped me, which is a lot worse than lying to someone."

Chloe shook her head. "I don't think so, Caroline. Kidnapping you was romantic; lying isn't."

"I'm afraid I'm not a romantic. Anyway, when I lied to him I barely knew him."

Chloe poured honey in her tea, then stirred the contents thoughtfully. "What about this Billy? How do you feel about him?"

"That's all over with. He seems like an old friend now."

"How did you feel about him when you were going with him?"

Caroline added some of the honey to her tea and found it improved the taste considerably. "You know, this isn't bad," she remarked.

"Stick to the subject. How did you feel about Billy?"

"I loved him in a way. Not anything like..."

"Not anything like what? Like Duffy?"

"No, but I don't love Duffy."

"I think you're just kidding yourself, Caroline. You just described to me an almost perfect weekend if you leave out the last part. And the two of you wouldn't have fought like that if you didn't care."

"I was right next door to loving him, Chloe, and could have crossed the line at any moment. But not now. The whole thing's too...too wearing. I have enough tension as a result of my job; I don't need it in my personal relationships too."

"Duffy's not going to give you up that easily, you know."

"That's where I think you're wrong. I hit him where it hurts, in his ego—a man like Duffy isn't going to stand for that."

"According to your horoscope—"

"Forget my horoscope! I'm in control of my life, not the stars, and certainly not Duffy. It's over, that's it, and I hope I never again meet another crazy man."

Chloe let out a long sigh. "Okay," she said at last. "Do you want to go to a movie?"

"Sure," agreed Caroline, thinking it would take her mind off the recent events. "What's playing?"

Chloe named a romantic comedy.

"Forget it."

"There's a science-fiction movie on Second Avenue."

"You're on," said Caroline. "Just let me change my clothes and I'll be right down."

Chloe was sifting through the leaves at the bottom of her cup as she left. *If she finds anything about Duffy in there,* Caroline vowed to herself, *I'm not even going to listen.*

Chapter Nine

The following week Caroline would look back on as the War of the Roses.

They started arriving in her office late Monday morning. The receptionist brought them in and gave them to Joyce, Caroline's secretary. Joyce, always discreet, didn't so much as glance at the attached card as she handed the long florist box to Caroline. She also didn't leave the office, but hovered at the door in case there were going to be confidences exchanged.

There weren't. Caroline dismissed her before taking the card out of the envelope. There was always the faint chance that Billy had arrived in town and sent them, but she didn't think it likely. The card was merely signed *Stephen Duffy*, no apology, no endearments. She opened the box and looked down at the dozen white roses. Why not red, she wondered, or yellow?

She carried the box out and placed it on Joyce's desk. "Find a vase for them, Joyce. You can keep them on your desk if you want. If you don't, just give them to Reception.''

"Is it your birthday?" Joyce asked, overcome by curiosity.

"No." She might have confided in Chloe, which in itself was against her nature, but she certainly wasn't going to confide in her secretary and have the details of her personal life spread around the office. She was still an enigma to them at this point and she wanted it to stay that way.

When Caroline returned from lunch, two dozen more had arrived. Joyce had arranged one dozen on her own desk and one on the windowsill in Caroline's office. Caroline marched out of her office with them and placed them on one of the tables in the reception area.

By late afternoon four more dozen had arrived and Joyce was told she didn't even want to hear of the arrival of any more roses, that she was personally in charge of getting rid of them in any way she saw fit. When one of the vice-presidents stopped by Caroline's office, a big smile on his face, Caroline stuck to business and didn't offer any excuse for the fact that the office was beginning to smell like a funeral parlor.

Shortly before five Joyce buzzed Caroline to tell her her fiancé was on the line.

"I have no fiancé," Caroline informed her. "Please get rid of whoever is on the line."

Moments later Joyce poked her blond head into

the office. "He says he'll pick you up for dinner at seven."

Caroline fixed her with a chilling gaze. "I thought I told you to get rid of him."

"But, Caroline, he sounded so nice," she offered as an excuse.

"Then you go to dinner with him!"

She called Chloe on the phone and told her of the latest development.

"I'm afraid it's my fault, Caroline. Duffy stopped by this morning wanting to know how he could fix things up between you two, and I told him it would be nice if he sent you roses and an apology."

"And he only took half of your advice."

"No apology?"

"Not a word. But many roses. Please, Chloe, no more advice like that. It's too late to fix things up and I'm simply not interested."

"What are you going to do about dinner tonight?"

"I'm going to work late. If you see Duffy again, tell him he's wasting his time."

"I told him Wednesday would be a more auspicious day."

"Forget auspicious days, Chloe. I did a lot of thinking about this last night and it would never work out with us. I'm not looking for romance, I'm looking for a promotion. I'll talk to you later, Chloe."

By six o'clock all the secretaries had gone home,

the phones had practically stilled, and Caroline was able to get some serious work done on several financial reports she was responsible for. The day had been distracting, just one more reason why she shouldn't be involved with a man. They always caused interruptions in one's life, taking one's mind off the business at hand.

By seven she was beginning to worry about what Duffy would do when he found she wasn't there for their dinner date. Knowing his track record, she was afraid of what she might expect. It wouldn't surprise her if at any moment she saw Duffy lowering himself on a window washer's device outside her office window and knocking to get in. Or perhaps calling in a bomb threat to the building? That had happened before, but usually during office hours when some perverse person had probably taken delight in seeing the large building being cleared of all personnel. The possibilities were endless; this man seemed capable of the most outrageous acts. Chloe would call them outrageously romantic, but Caroline felt *criminal* was a more definitive word.

A few minutes after seven she left the building and went to a nearby deli for a sandwich. She sat by the window where she could watch the entrance to her building. If she saw Duffy approaching the building she would be forewarned and could make her escape. Not that he'd be able to get up to her office; the security on the building was stringent.

She ate too fast, not even enjoying her food.

Duffy was upsetting her, but she didn't know how to put an end to it. Could she call in the police and charge him with harassment? Not likely. She doubted whether the police would consider roses as sufficient harassment, and it was a little late now to report the locking-in and kidnapping. If he kept this kind of thing up, however, it was going to end up with her looking ridiculous at the office and could jeopardize her job.

What she needed to do was to make some kind of decisive move that would effectively put an end to Duffy's romantic meanderings. And probably the only way to do that would be to find another man. And the only other man who came to mind was Billy. If Duffy saw that she was resuming her friendship with Billy, she was sure he would back off. His kind of ego would never permit another man in the picture.

Tomorrow morning she would call old friends in Houston and find out Billy's whereabouts. She was sure he'd help her out of this. Having come to a workable solution to her problem, she felt much better and was able to get a lot of work done when she returned to the office. At ten she figured it was safe to go home and felt pleased that three completed reports were now on her boss's desk for him to study in the morning.

She took a taxi home and was relieved to see that the lights were off in Duffy's shop. She didn't stop off to see Chloe, but went straight to her apartment. The phone was ringing when she let herself in, and continued ringing off and on as she undressed and showered. She finally unplugged it from the wall.

She was feeling very good about herself. She was acting in a businesslike manner, resisting Duffy's efforts to see her, putting any thoughts of romance right out of her mind. Once in bed, though, thoughts of Duffy pervaded her mind. It was far easier to dismiss him during the day; at night, alone in bed, she missed the closeness, the feel of his body next to her. She thought, *well, there's always Billy,* but then realized it wasn't just any body she wanted, only one.

Damn him for blowing into my life like some hurricane, she muttered, pounding on the pillow with her fists. She didn't think he was losing any sleep over this, unless he stayed up late at nights planning more and more devious schemes to ensnare her.

Tuesday was quiet, a lull in the storm. By noon she breathed a sign of relief that so far no more roses had arrived. By five, when no phone calls from a mythical fiancé had been received, she took off happily for the gym. She managed to get Billy's phone number in the city from the Oiler's coach, but it just might be that she wouldn't have to use it. She really didn't want to bring Billy into the picture unless absolutely necessary.

Disaster struck when she turned off Second Avenue and headed toward her apartment. Duffy's very large neon sign, which had once blazed out MURRAY HILL SECURITY, was now announcing to the world that DUFFY LOVES CAROLINE.

She stopped stock-still in the middle of the sidewalk and gazed at it in horror.

She immediately grew ten degrees warmer than the temperature outdoors, and if there was anything to the expression *seeing red*, she thought she was seeing it. This was public humiliation—something she wasn't going to tolerate for a moment. She could see, even from this distance, that the shop was dark and locked for the night, so she headed straight for Chloe's apartment.

Too angry to speak, Caroline walked past Chloe into the kitchen.

"You look like you could use something stronger than tea," said Chloe. "Bad day at the office?"

Caroline didn't know whether to laugh or cry. "Haven't you seen Duffy's sign?"

"Sign?"

"Yes, sign. His neon sign."

Chloe looked perplexed. "Sure I've seen his sign."

Caroline sat down at the table after tipping the chair free of cats. "His latest sign."

"Duffy has a new sign?"

"It would appear so."

"How about some vodka, Caroline?"

"Fine."

"With orange juice?"

"Straight."

"Oh, dear," murmured Chloe, pouring out some vodka for Caroline and some with juice for herself. "I'm almost afraid to ask what it says."

Caroline took the proffered glass and downed it. What would normally have stunned her, now seemed to have little or no effect. Her anger seemed to be stronger at the moment than alcohol. She beckoned to Chloe. "Come outside, I want you to see this."

Chloe followed along behind her and the two of them stood staring across the street.

"Can you believe that, Chloe?"

"I wish some man loved me that much."

"Chloe!"

"Well, I do. Roses, neon signs—you've got to admit it's romantic."

"It's an invasion of privacy!"

"Well, look at it this way—it could have been worse."

Caroline shook her head in resignation. "I fail to see how."

"He could have rented a billboard."

"That'll probably occur to him next." She turned away from the view, a picture of total dejection.

Chloe put her arm around Caroline's shoulders. "Come on—what you need is another drink."

"Or two."

"Right."

"Certainly there must be something I can do about this," said Caroline as Chloe refilled her glass. "That sign must be breaking some law."

"I don't think so. It's not against the law to put things like that in the *Village Voice*. I think it has to be libelous to be against the law. Now if the sign read 'Caroline loves Duffy,' then you might have him for something, but this one only says something about himself."

"Thank God I don't know anyone in the neighborhood; he's already making me look bad at the office."

"The easiest solution, Caroline, would be to just give in. You know you like him."

"Give in to his reign of terror? I don't care if that man takes out ads on TV and rents marching bands. He's got to learn that he can't have everything he wants."

"Even if you want it too?"

"The man is certifiably crazy. That is *not* what I want."

"I'd call it creative."

Caroline sat drinking the vodka, the alcohol finally beginning to numb her mind. But not enough to keep out thoughts of all the other things Duffy might do to her.

"I guess you think it's all my fault," came Chloe's small voice.

"Don't be silly."

"Well, in a way it is, you know. If I hadn't told you to call him when your apartment was broken into, and if I hadn't told him about your charts being perfectly matched, and if I hadn't suggested flowers..."

"Listen, Chloe, it's pointless to ruminate in the subjunctive. Anyway, I could do the same thing. If I hadn't moved to New York, if I hadn't gotten an apartment in this building—"

"That was my fault, too."

"And if I hadn't gone to bed with him."

"Yeah, I guess that wasn't my fault."

"I just wish there was some way I could retaliate, but I can't think of a thing."

"Oh, well, the most effective retaliation is what you're doing already—ignoring him. I don't think even Duffy will keep this up forever."

Caroline felt a momentary lifting of her spirits. "You really think so?"

"No. I was just trying to make you feel better."

"Nothing's going to make me feel better."

"Have you eaten?"

"No."

"How about going to McDonald's!"

Caroline gave her a halfhearted grin. "I was wrong. That would make me feel a little better."

Later, when she entered her apartment, the phone was once again ringing, and once again Caroline unplugged it from the wall. She walked over to the window to put on the air conditioner and couldn't help looking down and seeing the sign. DUFFY LOVES CAROLINE, blinking on and off, over and over, a never-ending reminder of the bane of her existence.

She turned on the TV to the end of a ball game and wouldn't have been able to tell the score when it was over. She was beginning to hate the city, hate her apartment, and hate men in general. She never thought of herself as a femme fatale, but she guessed there was no accounting for some men's tastes. It would probably be her misfortune to be pursued by him to the end of her days. She could at least be thankful for one thing. His outrageous behavior was beginning to blur her better memories of him and there were so many bad aspects of the situation to think about, she seldom remembered the good things.

If he had been smart and acted like a responsible adult, there might have been a chance of their getting back together. But not now. She'd never even consider it after this kind of irresponsible behavior. Good heavens, marry a man like that? She'd have to be as crazy as him to even consider it. One week of marriage to him would probably suffice to have her taken off to Bellevue in a straitjacket.

She watched the news, was relieved to see that a cold front was headed for New York, then went to bed. When sleep finally came, she dreamed of neon signs, all flashing on and off, all declaring to the world that Duffy loved Caroline.

In the morning Duffy was in front of his shop when she headed out of the building for her run. She immediately backtracked, spending the next forty minutes running in place in her living room. It was a bad start to the day.

On the other hand, the temperature and humidity had dropped overnight and the day had a feeling of fall about it. She decided to leave early and walk to work. She did what she had noticed thousands of other women in the city doing: She wore her running shoes with her dress and carried her heels in her purse. It made for some odd-looking outfits, her own as well, but also made for a much easier walk and happier feet.

The roses resumed that day. Only the color had changed, this time they were red. Along with the first florist box came a rather large envelope, inside of which was a Polaroid picture of Duffy's new sign. He must have thought it possible that she had missed seeing it, although only a blind person could have missed it. She tore the picture up and threw it in the wastebasket, then relegated the flowers to the reception area where the white ones were already beginning to droop.

By noon, when her "fiancé" had called for the first time, six dozen had already been delivered and the receptionist was frantically trying to find containers to hold them all. Caroline told Joyce to tell her "phony fiancé" that she was out of town on a business trip, and could tell by Joyce's curt answer that she didn't approve of the way her boss treated men. She found she could no longer concentrate on her work after that and left the office.

Instead of lunch, she walked around Saks looking at winter coats. She'd never needed a winter coat before, or boots or mufflers or any of the other accoutrements of snowy winters. The furs were lovely, but she wasn't sure she believed in killing animals just to keep warm, and furthermore couldn't afford them even if she did. The down coats looked terrific on the racks but on her seemed large and ungainly. She had a feeling no one under six feet tall could successfully wear a down coat. Which left only wool, and they weren't interesting at all.

She finally saw something called a storm coat. It looked like a raincoat but had a furry lining, and the saleswoman assured her it was just the thing for snow. Caroline charged it and made arrangements to have it delivered, then left the store and headed back to work.

More roses had arrived in her absence. Joyce was out to lunch but had left a message on her desk that Duffy had called again and asked if she was planning on spending the weekend with him on Staten Island. She did not look forward to the looks she was sure to receive from Joyce after that message.

There was a department meeting that afternoon where an upcoming trip to Dubai was discussed. Sensing that she might be the one chosen to make the trip, she decided to work later again that night and get up-to-date on all her reports. There was competition within the department for the next opening of vice-president, and she wanted to make certain she was in the running.

At about eight that night she was alone in the

office when a call came from the security guard in the lobby informing her that a Mr. Duffy was downstairs and was asking permission to come up.

"No, Frank, I'm not seeing anyone tonight," Caroline told the guard, hoping that Duffy wouldn't make a scene in the lobby. She heard no more from Frank and was beginning to relax, only to look up and find Duffy standing in the doorway to her office, a shopping bag at his side.

"How did you get in here?" Caroline hissed at him, noticing at the same time how handsome he looked in a gray suit and tie.

"I believe it was my American Express card, although it could have been my Visa."

"How did you get past the guard?"

"I just waited until he was busy on the phone."

"Well, you can just get out of here now. I don't want your roses or your telephone messages or you. As for that sign—"

He grinned broadly. "Adds a touch of class to the neighborhood, don't you think?"

"I think it's presumptuous and despicable. You're making me the laughingstock of the neighborhood and the office and if you don't desist I'm going to have to seek legal recourse."

"I'm not breaking any laws; I already checked it out with John."

"What about breaking in here?"

He walked over to her desk and set the shopping bag on top of it. "Go on, call the guard and have him throw me out."

She sat there seething with rage. He knew exactly what to do to get his way. She couldn't possibly call Frank and have this whole episode on record. Everything he did seemed to be calculated to make her look bad.

He reached into the bag and cartons of Chinese food began to appear on her desk. "I figured since we missed the Chinese dinner the other night that I ought to make up for it," he said cheerfully.

"Just get out of my office, Duffy!"

He handed her a paper plate, chopsticks, and a napkin, then set out his own on the other side of the desk. Pulling up a chair, he began to eat. Caroline hadn't eaten at all that day and could have devoured the food in five minutes flat, but was certainly not going to give him the satisfaction.

"Your office looks just like your apartment," he remarked.

She folded her arms across her chest and ignored him.

"Just as businesslike, just as impersonal. Don't you like roses?"

"That depends on who sent them."

"Your secretary sounds friendly and nice."

"Then send roses to my secretary."

"And incur your jealousy? I wouldn't think of it."

"Go to hell!"

He gave her a level glance. "Look, Caroline, I forgive you, okay? Why don't we just start again?"

"*You* forgive *me*?"

"I suppose you had your reasons for lying to me. I don't like it, but if we start over and base our relationship on truth this time instead of lies, I think I could live with it."

She got up from the desk and turned her back to him. The view out of the window was magic: All the lights were going on in the city, turning it into a fairyland. She knew she had to do something, something that would infuriate him to the point where he would leave. If he didn't leave, she just didn't trust herself alone with him. Already, angry as she was with him, she was longing to walk around the desk and throw herself into his arms. What a precarious situation it was when you hated the man you longed for.

She turned around and faced him. "I've decided to go back with Billy," she told him.

His expression never changed. "I don't blame you, Caroline. He's a good ball player, good-looking guy. Probably makes lots of money."

"He also doesn't do asinine things like having signs made up to embarrass me."

He gave her an innocent look. "Were you embarrassed? I thought you'd be pleased. I figured I was immortalizing our love."

"*Your* love."

"*Our* love."

"I realized, after I left you Sunday, that I'm still in love with Billy. Now that we're both in New York…"

He was out of his chair and walking around the

desk toward her and Caroline began to panic. She thought of circling around the other side of the desk, keeping the large piece of furniture between them, but then she'd be acting as childishly as he acted. She stood her ground, but it was no solution at all because he was putting his arms around her and pulling her close.

"Sure you're still in love with Billy," he said, looking down at her with laughing eyes. "That's why you get so excited whenever I get close to you. That's why you were so passionate with me in bed. It's obvious you still love Billy."

Her best shot and it hadn't worked! She tried to stiffen her body to resist him, but it didn't work. Like a magnet her body was drawn to his, which so dismayed her she felt tears of frustration threatening behind her lids. He was leaning down to kiss her now and at the very last moment as her own lips met his, a new strategy occurred to her.

"I have a business proposition to make to you, Duffy," she said, her voice sounding hoarse to her ears.

His head stopped its descent. "I'm listening."

"Stop the roses, stop the phone calls purporting to be my fiancé, get rid of the sign—"

"And?"

"And we'll have a relationship based on sex."

He stood back from her and placed his hands on her shoulders. "Just sex?"

She nodded.

"No friendship?"

"That didn't seem to work out."

"Sorry, Caroline, I'm not interested. Why should I settle for that when I can have it all?"

"Because you can't have it all!"

He reached out for her again, this time fastening his mouth over hers and showing her he could indeed have it all if he could keep getting her alone. She melted against him, caught up in the kiss. She cursed her body for giving in so easily, but her heart wasn't in it. She was pressing against him, her lips parting, when he stepped back from her, leaving her leaning against the window for support.

"Come along, let's eat. The food's getting cold. We can continue this later."

Be calm, Caroline, she exhorted herself. *Don't let him see how he gets to you. Let him think you're acquiescing and then get out of his reach at the first opportunity.*

She smiled at him and sat down behind her desk, reaching to put portions of the food onto her plate. He looked satisfied, at ease, deftly lifting the food with his chopsticks.

"Where's the tea?" Caroline asked him.

"Sorry, I guess they forgot about it."

"Would you like me to make some?"

"You have it here?"

She nodded.

"Sure—that would be great."

"Be back in a second," she said, sorry that she couldn't get her purse out of her desk drawer. But that would surely alert him.

She left her office, went down the hall, crossed the reception area and was out and waiting for an elevator in under a minute. She had no money and would have to walk home, but that didn't bother her. Her hunger was beginning to bother her, but not enough to sit and eat Chinese food with the enemy.

Once on the street she practically ran the first two blocks, not really slowing down until she reached Lexington Avenue. Hungry, with no money and afraid to go home in case Duffy was there, she walked for hours. When she finally got home it was after eleven and her street looked deserted. She had to buzz Chloe to let her in, then stand by while she picked the lock to her door. If she hadn't been in such a hurry to leave the office she would have made sure she at least had her keys with her.

The telephone was ringing when she got inside and she unplugged it before going to the kitchen to see if there was anything edible. All there was was a box of Frosted Flakes and no milk to go with them. She took the box anyway and began to eat them dry.

She found Billy's phone number in her wallet, plugged in the phone and dialed. He answered on the first ring.

"Billy?"

"Is that you, Carrie?"

She nodded in relief, then realized he couldn't hear a nod. "Yes, it's me."

"Where have you been? I've been calling you every night, but no one ever answers."

"It's a long story, Billy. Listen, I need your help."

"You've got it, honey. What can I do for you?"

Just when she felt the world and Duffy were conspiring against her, it was wonderful to feel she had someone in her corner. "Could you come over tomorrow night, Billy? I'll get in some Chinese food and we can eat and talk."

"Be glad to take you out to dinner."

"No, I'd rather you came here."

"Anything you say, Carrie."

She gave him her address, directions on how to get there, then listened for a few minutes as Billy told her about the Jets' chances that season. When they finally hung up she was feeling better than she had felt for days.

Maybe Duffy didn't believe her threats about Billy, but when he saw him in person he'd have to believe it. And Billy in person was pretty hard to miss.

She got the best night's sleep she'd had in days.

Chapter Ten

The strange look the receptionist gave her in the morning Caroline attributed to the possible arrival of yet more roses. Joyce, however, was trying to stifle the giggles, and Caroline wondered, her heart dropping to her stomach, whether Duffy had had the effrontery to camp out in her office.

All traces of the Chinese food were gone, but on her window, and the first thing one saw when entering the office, was a large heart with an arrow running through it—the words "Duffy loves Caroline" easily read. It appeared to be written in lipstick—her lipstick. And it probably looked to Joyce as though Caroline had written it.

She took a handful of tissues from the box on her desk and tried to erase it. She obliterated the words, but the window remained a smeary mess. She didn't say a word when Joyce entered her office with a bottle of Windex and some paper towels, just hoped that none of the men in the office had seen it.

There were no telephone calls that day, no roses. She wondered if it was another lull before the storm and she could expect something even worse than a neon sign when she arrived home.

There were rumors floating around the office that she'd be the one picked to go to Dubai to deal with the affiliate Arab oil company there. She was kept busy all day with meetings and reports and telephone calls, but in between she sandwiched in thoughts about the wardrobe she would take with her if she was picked. She thought the Arab businessmen would probably consider pants too blatantly liberated, while on the other hand dresses would probably be considered too revealing. One thing was for sure: She was not about to wear a veil, even if it meant more successful business dealings.

Shortly after five she left the office and stopped off at a Chinese restaurant on Third Avenue for some takeout food. She picked up enough for three. It might not be a bad idea to have Chloe up for a bite to eat. The reunion with Billy might become a little sticky if they were alone in the apartment. Chloe could serve as chaperone and might even offer a few suggestions on the new game plan Caroline was planning to put into effect.

She called Chloe when she got home and invited her up, then changed into jeans and a Houston Oiler sweatshirt for the occasion. It had been a gift from Billy: He liked to see her wearing it in the seats reserved for the players' wives and girlfriends at the games.

Chloe arrived in a flowing purple caftan, gold sandals on her feet. Her hair had been cut and now resembled a rusty Brillo pad. Purple feathers dangled from her ears.

"So what's new in the battle between the sexes?" she asked, helping Caroline set out the food on the table.

Caroline recounted the previous evening's events, ending up with the lipstick heart on her window. She then told Chloe about Billy and what she had in mind.

"Another man—good thinking. If Duffy sees you with another guy he's sure to back off."

"My thoughts exactly."

"How are you going to feel, though, if you see Duffy with another woman?"

"Relieved," said Caroline, not believing it for a moment. She didn't think this was likely to happen, though. If Duffy started seeing someone else she doubted whether they'd be hanging around his shop together. And what she didn't see could hardly bother her. She had never been jealous by nature; she just didn't want it flaunted in her face.

"Maybe he'll keep the new sign but just keep changing the woman's name."

"Sounds like his style," said Caroline, and was about to go on when the buzzer sounded and she hit the button to let Billy into the building.

Moments later he was standing in the door. She had forgotten how his presence seemed to fill the room. Literally fill the room. At six foot five and two hundred and twenty-five pounds, he seemed to dwarf her apartment. She had a brief glimpse of thick blond hair and a mouthful of teeth that would have made an orthodontist proud, and then he was hugging her tightly against the familiar bulk of his body.

She had forgotten how beautiful he was and his easy, uncomplicated, comfortable presence. "Billy," she said, breaking away from him and leading him into the room by the hand, "I want you to meet my friend, Chloe."

Chloe, mouth agape, was looking at him in wide-eyed wonder. "I guess it's true about Texans," she murmured, reaching out to shake his hand. "What sign are you?"

"Sign?"

"She wants to know your birth date, Billy," Caroline interpreted.

"April ninth," said Billy.

"The ram," said Chloe. "That could be interesting."

"Not a Ram, a Jet," Billy told her.

Chloe was looking confused. "They're football teams, Chloe," Caroline informed her. "Billy's now with the New York Jets."

"I don't know anything about football, I'm afraid," Chloe said, her eyes still fastened on Billy with wonder.

"A little lady as pretty as you doesn't need to know," said Billy, his Southern gallantry surfacing.

Chloe was blushing, her eyes now downcast, and

Caroline was about to say, "Give me a break, you two," knowing Chloe to be a liberated woman and Billy to be the kind of ball player who eschewed anyone who couldn't talk football with him. Then she took a second look at them and saw that she just might have a budding romance on her hands. Her ex-lover and new friend couldn't seem to take their eyes off each other.

"Let's eat, folks," said Caroline, then watched as Billy pulled Chloe's chair out for her and Chloe didn't even protest. "Maybe you could teach her about football," she said to Billy, and he immediately replied that it would be his pleasure.

Billy started talking football to Chloe and it carried Caroline back to previous dinner conversations with Billy. He never arugued, rarely even discussed. He mostly provided information relating to football, most of which Caroline could have read in the newspapers. It had a soothing, calming effect, and probably made for better digestion. It was also extremely boring and she wondered why she had never realized that before. He was comfortable to be with and easy to get along with, but with Billy life had lacked any excitement. Part of it was that he was so predictable, unlike some people she could mention but would prefer not to. However, that was why she had invited him to dinner and it was time to get the show on the road.

"I'm having a little problem, Billy," she inserted in the first lull in the conversation.

"That's right, you said something about that over the phone. What can I do to help?"

"Well, there's this man who's bothering me—"

"I'll kill him!"

"No, Billy, nothing that drastic." She went on to tell him the rudiments of her relationship with Duffy, and unlike Chloe he wasn't laughing at the more amusing parts.

"That kind of behavior would get him killed down in Texas," Billy said when she was finished. "He doesn't sound like any kind of gentleman to me."

"He's really a very nice person," Chloe told him.

"Well, if you say so, little lady, I guess I'll have to take that for fact."

Little lady? Had he used to refer to her that way? Caroline couldn't remember, but hoped she hadn't put up with that. Caroline was beginning to wonder what she had ever seen in him, aside from the fact that he was a very good person.

Whatever it was, though, Chloe seemed to be seeing it now. "He's really in love with her, Billy, only I guess Caroline just isn't ready for that yet."

"Carrie never was the marrying kind," said Billy, causing Caroline to wonder why he had proposed to her in that case. Maybe he had felt safe in assuming her answer would be no.

"What do you want me to do, Carrie? Just name it," Billy was saying.

"I thought you could play the part of the other man for me."

"That'll only make him jealous."

"No, I think it will make him back off, and that's what I want. Also, he knows about you, so us getting back together again would look natural."

The telephone rang and Chloe looked from Caroline to Billy. "If that's him, you ought to have Billy answer the phone."

Caroline was starting to nod her head in agreement and Billy took it as a sign to answer the phone. He picked it up, said a gruff hello, then handed it to Caroline. All of which didn't help matters at all; she should just have unplugged it to begin with.

"Who was that?" came Duffy's familiar voice.

"Oh, that was Billy," she said casually, as though Billy were always there to answer her phone.

"No kidding? I'd like to meet him," said Duffy. "I'll be right over." And before she could tell him she didn't want to see him, he had hung up.

"Did it work?" asked Chloe.

"Hardly—he's on his way over. Says he wants to meet Billy."

Billy smiled expansively. "Now don't you two little ladies worry. There's not going to be any fighting, any rough stuff. You just leave the handling of this guy to me."

"What are you going to do, Billy?" Caroline asked him.

"Just discuss the situation with him like a gentleman and persuade him to back off."

"Duffy's no gentleman," muttered Caroline.

"All the more reason why I should handle it for you. Just remember to act like you like me while he's here."

"I do like you, Billy."

"You know what I mean, Carrie."

The thought of Duffy's imminent arrival put a harness on Caroline's appetite. She was starting to worry about what would happen when the two men met, but she didn't have long to worry as Duffy arrived almost immediately. The buzzer from the lobby didn't sound, so when the knock came at the door she could only assume he had picked the lock downstairs.

He was wearing jeans and a sweatshirt and he either needed a shave or was trying to grow a beard. For some reason this made him look even sexier than usual. She deftly evaded his embrace, and headed back to the table, introducing him to Billy on the way.

Billy was on his feet in the manner of a proper Texas gentleman and had his hefty hand out to shake Duffy's.

"Billy Tyler," said Duffy, as though he couldn't believe his good luck in seeing him there, "this is a real pleasure. I've been following your career ever since you played with Southern Methodist."

Billy instantly melted into boyish good humor, evidently forgetting the purpose of the meeting.

"Yeah? Well, I'm hoping you'll follow it with the Jets now."

"They're my team," said Duffy, "and I was sure pleased when I heard you'd been traded. How do you feel about the opener with the Raiders?"

Pleased when he heard it? Caroline recalled just how pleased he had been and felt like saying so, but already Duffy had sat down at the table and was making himself completely at home. Chloe had even gotten up to get him a plate, and he was digging into the Chinese food as though he had been invited to dinner.

"This seems to be the week for Chinese food," Duffy said to Caroline with a wink, then went back to his conversation with Billy. He either really was a fan of Billy's or he had researched the subject in case of just such an eventuality. He was giving a play-by-play description of some bowl game he had seen Billy in several years before, and for once Billy was enthralled enough to listen.

After about twenty minutes of being bored to death with their buddy-buddy behavior, Caroline caught Chloe's eye across the table and they exchanged grimaces.

"Would you like to see my new winter coat?" she asked Chloe, and it wasn't even noticed when the two of them left the room.

"So much for Billy's handling the situation," she said, trying on the coat for Chloe.

"He's some hunk," breathed Chloe, a look of near rapture on her face.

"Billy?"

"You got it."

"I thought you two seemed to be hitting it off."

"You really think so? You think it was mutual?"

"I'm sure of it. And he's a nice guy, Chloe—I highly recommend him."

"You don't mind?"

"Why should I mind?"

"I thought maybe you'd want to get back together with him now that you're dumping Duffy."

"You know that's just a ploy to get rid of Duffy."

"But he's so beautiful!"

"He's all yours—yours and all those groupies football players seem to acquire. Well, what do you think?"

"I think I'm in love."

"I mean the coat. Do you like it?"

"Sure, those kind are great in the snow."

Caroline took off the coat and hung it back up in the closet. "I think we'd better get back in there and break up the huddle. And listen, Chloe—I'll make sure Billy gets your telephone number."

"Got any beer, Carrie?" asked Billy as soon as they entered the room.

"Sure. How about you, Duffy?"

"A beer would be great."

"Chloe?"

"If you have any more of that wine..."

Caroline got out the beer and wine while Chloe cleared off the table. The men had moved to the couch and Billy was now diagraming plays for

Duffy while Duffy looked on in seeming admiration. She felt like calling to order the first meeting of the Billy Tyler fan club.

"Billy, darling," Caroline finally said, "didn't you want to make the last movie?"

Billy looked at her as though she were speaking a foreign language.

"You two were going to the movies, remember?" Chloe chimed in.

Caroline saw the look of amusement on Duffy's face as it finally dawned on Billy what he was there for.

"Sorry, sweetheart, but I'm afraid tonight's off. I have practice in the morning and I have to get to bed early. We'll make it Friday night instead, okay?"

Caroline was forced to acquiesce sweetly, and even walked by Billy and ruffled his hair with her hand. Rather than make Duffy jealous, he immediately went into a fit of coughing to mask the laugh that had erupted from his throat. Caroline had an urge to strangle that same throat.

Billy finally wound up his football talk at about ten o'clock and then, as though suddenly remembering, told Duffy he hoped he didn't mind that he was seeing Caroline again.

"Not at all," said Duffy expansively. "I can see she's in good hands."

"That's real nice of you to see it that way," said Billy, "I think Carrie was afraid there was going to be some fuss."

"*Carrie* thought that?"

"You know how women are," said Billy. "But I was sure we could come to some agreement."

"No problem," said Duffy. "I defer to the better man."

"No, it's not like that at all. You seem like a real straight guy, Duffy. It's just that...well, I was there first."

"Right. You scored the first touchdown."

"Damn right. You kind of took over while I was on the sidelines, but now I'm back in the lineup."

Duffy stood up and shook Billy's hand. "Good luck on the extra points, Billy."

Furious at being discussed like a football game, Caroline was more than ready to show them both the door. Billy beat her to it by saying good-bye to Caroline, belatedly remembering to kiss her good-bye at the door. Chloe left with the men and Caroline was left feeling left out by all of them.

She kicked off her shoes, sat down at the table and poured herself a glass of wine. It looked as though her two friends were going to desert her for each other, leaving her to cope with Duffy all by herself. Why couldn't the man behave like an adult? Why did he have to be a continual source of irritation to her? If he had ever behaved in a halfway rational manner they just might have made a good couple. They could have had a lot going for them, but instead he had to turn a burgeoning relationship into a farce. She could only hope she'd get the business trip to Dubai. Maybe out of sight out of mind would work in this case. She had a lot of doubts that using Billy as a decoy was going to work.

When a knock came at the door she was sure it was Chloe wanting more information on Billy. She opened the door and instead found Duffy standing there. He quickly brushed by her and entered the room.

"How about a glass of that for me, Carrie?"

"No. And don't call me Carrie. And please leave."

"Thrilled to see me, I see," he said, pouring himself some wine in Chloe's glass and lifting it to her before drinking.

She leaned back against the front door, wanting to stay as far out of his grasp as possible. "Why don't you give it up and go home, Duffy?"

"Give it up? You mean you? I thought of it, Carrie, I really did, but Billy's much too nice for you."

"So nice he's going to come up here and punch you in the nose."

"Don't hold your breath—the last I saw of him he was going into Chloe's apartment to get his horoscope charted."

His smug tone was infuriating. "Why can't you just accept the fact Billy and I are back together again and leave me alone?"

"Believe me, if I had seen evidence of it I would. Instead I saw you and Billy acting mostly indifferent to each other, and Billy and Chloe hitting it off. And even though you're standing way the hell over there, I can still feel the electricity between us."

"What you feel is my anger, and you're completely wrong about me and Billy. We're thinking quite seriously of living together."

He got up from the table and began to walk toward her. "You want me to prove here and now what a lie that is?"

She managed to circle him, ending up by the windows. "I just want you to leave me alone."

"Couldn't we sit down and talk this over like adults?" he asked in a reasonable manner, as though he weren't the one who was childish. He came up beside her and glanced out the window. "Isn't that romantic?" he asked, referring to the ignominious sign flashing on an off across the street.

She flinched as she looked down at the sign, then went and sat down at the table. "All right, Duffy, let's discuss this like adults. You're embarrassing the hell out of me at the office and possibly even jeopardizing my job. You'd be making me the laughingstock of the neighborhood if anyone knew me, which, thank God, they don't. You have come into my life, continuously disrupted it, and are managing to cause me mental anguish. I live in constant fear of what you will do next. Isn't there any way I can get you to stop all this?"

He sat down across from her and grinned. "Sure. You can marry me."

"Isn't there any way short of marrying you?"

He shook his head. "I can't think of any."

"God, you're so stupid. Do you really want to marry someone who doesn't want to marry you?"

"I think you do want to marry me. On Sunday the only thing that seemed to be holding you back was some future chance of being transferred. We could have worked that out."

"Until you flew off the handle."

"We both flew off the handle. You can't keep running away from your problems, Caroline."

"The only problem I have is you. And I find it far preferable to run away from you than to marry you. Can't you get it through that thick skull of yours that I don't happen to want to get married? Aren't the statistics in New York something like three million unmarried women to one million unmarried men? Something like that?"

"I think that's about right."

"Then why me? I can't believe I'm one in a million, let alone one in three million. Can't you find someone else to harass? Furthermore, I'm not the least interested in moving to the suburbs, learning to cook and having two-point-four, or whatever it is, children."

"You don't have to worry about that. I wouldn't want someone with your views bringing up my children."

"See? I'm right. We're not suited and you wouldn't be happy married to me so can't we just forget the whole thing? Just pretend you never met me, Duffy, and I'll gladly do the same." She was seething at the thought that he didn't think her fit to bring up his children. Not that she wanted to, of course, nor would she want his criminal views of how to do things foisted on her children, should she have any. She pictured a little boy looking very much like a miniature Duffy locking his little sister up in her bedroom. Any children Duffy might have would probably turn out to be monsters.

"I'm afraid that's impossible," said Duffy, breaking into her daydream and bringing her back to reality. "I'm in love with you and the campaign shall continue until I win." He poured them each some more wine and held up his glass. "To victory!"

Caroline pushed her glass out of the way and lowered her head onto the table. She covered her face with her arms as her body began to shake.

Duffy was instantly on his feet and by her side, his hand going out to pat her gently on the back. "Hey, don't cry, Caroline, I didn't mean to upset you. Everything's going to be all right, I promise."

She jerked her head up and pushed away his arm. "I wasn't crying, you fool," she managed to say, still laughing. "I just figured your next move would be to smash the glass against the wall and I didn't want to see it. Now will you get the hell out of here and leave me alone?"

Duffy was suddenly all innocence. "I'm going, I'm going. You get a good night's sleep, honey, and I'll talk to you tomorrow."

"You will not talk to me tomorrow!"

"Then I'll talk to your secretary, what's her name? Joyce, isn't it?"

"Just get out," she ordered, each word measured.

She got up and walked ahead of him, making a point of opening the door wide and gesturing toward the hall. "Good night, Mr. Duffy."

He leaned down and planted a kiss on her mouth. She could feel herself waver then, and knew that he did too, because he pulled her against him and proceeded to kiss her with considerably more passion. And her body, her nemesis when it came to Duffy, once again betrayed her by moving in against him and fitting itself to his. At which point Duffy backed off.

"No, Caroline, no sex. I know you want it, and so do I, but I've decided to wait until we're married. I don't want to be merely a sex object to you."

Caroline was too furious to speak. Now the idiot was holding out for marriage? Well, that was fine with her, it had only been a momentary lapse anyway. And if he wasn't going to use sex to get her, he was abandoning his most powerful weapon. He certainly wasn't going to get her with silly pranks. Angrier than she could ever remember being, Caroline shoved him out into the hall and slammed the door. She could hear his laugh as he walked away.

She had always wanted to come to New York, had actually thought she'd enjoy living here. Now she was seriously considering asking for a transfer to someplace where the inhabitants were sane. And where she would be able to maintain her sanity.

"Do you want to move again, Charlie?" she asked, speaking to her moose head.

Charlie didn't reply.

Chapter Eleven

If Duffy was Napoleon going forth to do battle, then Thursday was surely the day he should have been banished to Elba. She had somehow reckoned that Duffy had done his worst, but her own personal Waterloo came the following morning.

Everything had been near perfect up until the "event." The weather was in the low seventies and dry and she was able to run her six miles without seeing Duffy either going or coming. Within moments of reaching her office Joyce had her coffee and cheese Danish on the desk. One of her co-workers stopped by for a chat and let drop the news that she was almost a sure thing for the trip to Dubai. The phone was blessedly silent; no more roses arrived to embellish the office. And then, shortly before eleven, disaster struck.

She saw a movement in her doorway and looked up from the papers she was working on to see a giant fake chicken standing in her doorway. When the chicken started to move she realized that it was a person dressed up like a chicken and then all thought ceased as the chicken opened up its mouth and began to sing.

In a rather professional voice, the chicken proceeded to sing a rousing rendition of "Sweet Caroline," a song that had been vastly popular in Caroline's youth. She had even, in fact, owned a recording of it at one time.

As she watched the chicken sing in shocked silence, she was subliminally aware of the crowd gathered around the door to her office. There was Joyce and the receptionist and soon there was practically everyone connected to the company with the possible exception of Mr. Bonnard, the comptroller, who was rumored never to leave his office even for lunch. As curious faces peered in, some of them laughing, all of them at least smiling, the chicken sang on and on. At one point he even attempted to tap dance, but his soft chicken feet on the carpeting seemed to slow him down so he finally settled for wiggling his fat body and waving his wings about.

If Caroline had still been in California she would have prayed for an earthquake. As it was, it took all her control not to sink down in her chair and ultimately hide beneath her desk. She felt herself flushing scarlet and a sweat breaking out all over her, but she seemed powerless to do anything but just sit and watch and listen as that dreadful chicken sang its little heart out. At the end, and blessedly there was an end, the chicken piped up in a little chicken chirp, "With love from Duffy."

The chicken departed and Caroline watched as Joyce shooed everyone away from her office and then thoughtfully closed the door. But why, oh why, hadn't she shooed away the chicken to begin with? Caroline, who hadn't cried since she was eight years old and fallen out of a tree, and those tears had been of anger over losing a bet over who could climb the highest, put her head down on the desk and cried tears of frustration.

She was certain it was only a matter of time before the ax came down and she was fired. Had any other budding executive ever had a visit from a chicken during office hours? A chicken who sang while all the oil company personnel stood around agape, and then announced a little personal message? She thought not. She was rather sure it was a first, and not a first that would go unnoticed.

She didn't emerge from her office until noon, and then, head down, walked quickly to the bank of elevators and escaped the building as though escaping from a fire.

After lunch there was a department meeting that Caroline was obliged to attend. If she had had any Valium at hand she would have taken one, or perhaps the whole bottle and thus avoid the meeting entirely. She was the last one to arrive and all heads at the long table turned to her as she made her entrance. She paused momentarily in the doorway, thoughts of fleeing filling her head. She could always return to California and try to get another job, one where her co-workers' heads wouldn't be filled with images of chickens whenever she appeared. And then one of the men began to hum "Sweet Caroline" under his breath, but the silence in the room was such that it could be heard. Soon another took up the melody, and then another, and soon the room was filled with the sounds of "Sweet Caroline" and it was easily as bad as one of those nightmares where you suddenly appear in the middle of crowded Main Street in your nightgown, having no idea how you got there.

And then, just when she thought she could take it no more, the men burst into good-natured laughter and there were shouts of, "Hey, Caroline, don't take it so hard, it happens to the best of us," and other such words to put her at her ease. Her boss even admitted to getting obscene phone calls from a strange woman only to find out during the fourth such call that it had been a wrong number all the time and it had been *his* boss she had wanted.

"There are a lot of nuts in this city," one of the men confided, "you just happened to meet up with yours early."

Caroline gradually relaxed during the meeting and men she had hardly spoken to before commiserated with her like old friends. When it was finally announced that Caroline would represent the company in Dubai in two weeks' time, there was applause around the table followed by more good-natured ribbing on how to handle herself with the Arab men.

Her secretary was as excited as Caroline by the news. "Oh, I wish I could go with you—those Arab men are so romantic," she enthused, not bothering to listen when Caroline reminded her the trip was purely business. "Not that Duffy isn't romantic," she hastened to add. "I mean, sending a singing chicken, that was really adorable, wasn't it? I wish my boyfriend would send me a chicken."

"If another chicken or any other kind of oddity shows up at the office, please don't allow it in, Joyce."

"I tried to stop it, Caroline, honest, but that was one stubborn chicken. Anyway, everyone wanted to see what he would do. You're not mad, are you?"

"Mad" didn't even begin to describe how Caroline felt about that particular chicken. In a way, though, it had done her some good. A couple of men admitted to her after the meeting that while previously she had seemed to them rather stand-offish, now they considered her one of the guys. Caroline's natural reticence dissolved somewhat at the news. She would have to start being more friendly to the men she worked with. Perhaps she should suggest lunch to them on occasion or even a drink after work. If they had been women she knew she would have done it much sooner.

Knowing the stores were open late on Thursday nights, Caroline stopped by Saks after work with clothes for her trip in mind. There were lots of fall cotton which was just what she needed. She bought a couple of suits in dark colors and decided to leave the skirts long for the trip and have them shortened on her return. She bought several high-necked, long-sleeved blouses and one pair of sturdy low heels. She liked to pack lightly for trips and decided if she needed anything else while she was there, she would buy it in Dubai.

She stopped by Chloe's apartment when she got home to tell her about the chicken debacle and found Billy ensconced in the kitchen drinking green tea, which she was sure was a first for him.

The two of them broke up at her account of the singing/dancing chicken and it was minutes before Chloe was able to say, "I know that chicken."

"What do you mean you know him?"

"He stands around Twenty-third Street to advertise Kentucky Fried Chicken. I even talked to him one day. He's been in a few Broadway musicals, in the chorus, but most of the time he works as a chicken. You're lucky he didn't send a stripper/singer—they have those for rent, you know."

Caroline didn't even want to think about the reaction a stripper/singer would have received at her office. "I think it's time to put our plan into action," Caroline told Billy. "How about going out to dinner?"

They agreed that Caroline and Billy would leave the building together and Chloe would join them a few minutes later. Since Billy hadn't seen much of the city since his arrival they decided to take him to the Village.

The charade didn't turn out to be successful as Duffy wasn't around to see Billy and Caroline leave the building together. The Italian restaurant on Christopher Street was successful, though, and afterward Billy's size and good looks made a distinct impression on the inhabitants of Greenwich Village, most of them male. Billy merely thought they were football fans who recognized him until Chloe set him straight.

They walked through Washington Square Park after dinner and watched the roller skaters and musicians for a while and then stopped to have a drink at one of the sidewalk cafés before walking home. Chloe and Billy held hands and their strong attraction for each other was evident. Chloe confided that their charts weren't particularly compatible, but added that she was beginning to think astrology was nonsense, anyway. Caroline told her she had known that all along.

Caroline said good night to them in the lobby and went up to her apartment. She was conditioned now to expect the worst, but there were no further surprises in her apartment and the phone didn't even ring that night. She had only Friday to get through before the weekend, and if it was at all possible she'd try to get out of town, and out of reach, over the weekend. Perhaps Billy and Chloe could be persuaded to rent a car and drive to Cape Cod for a couple of days. She'd be able to relax out of Duffy's reach and maybe get her head together about the whole affair.

She watched the news at eleven, then made an early night of it.

In the morning she met Billy coming out of Chloe's apartment when she got downstairs to run. He gave her a sheepish grin when she said good morning, and she assured him she was pleased at how their romance was progressing.

"She's different, Caroline, I've never met anyone like her."

"No one's ever met anyone like Chloe, she's one of a kind," she said, and Billy nodded in agreement.

As they stepped out of the building together Caroline saw Duffy across the street unlocking the door to his shop.

"Quick," she said to Billy, "put your arms around me and kiss me good-bye."

Faster on his feet than usual, Billy instantly complied with her request, and feeling very foolish Caroline stood in the middle of the sidewalk locked in Billy's embrace while pedestrians walked around them. She kept her eyes open during the kiss and saw to her satisfaction that Duffy was witnessing the entire scene. And he didn't look pleased. She was sure that if Chloe was watching out the window she'd understand the situation.

Calling out a cheery good-bye to Billy, Caroline started off running toward Third Avenue. She suddenly felt ten pounds lighter as though a weight

had fallen from her. Duffy was certain to miscon-
strue the scene and assume Billy and she had spent
the night together. She was absolutely certain that
this was something he wouldn't tolerate. Even normal men were unduly posessive; Duffy's posses-
siveness probably assumed criminal proportions.

She was still congratulating herself when she
reached the office and things couldn't have gone
more smoothly that day. No roses, no phone calls,
no chickens, nothing but peace and quiet, and she
even had lunch with some of the men in her group.
They gave her tips on how to behave in Dubai:
Don't smoke, don't even mention the word alcohol, don't flirt, don't dress immodestly—don't,
don't, don't! None of which bothered her in the
least. If she could handle the business with Duffy,
she could handle anything.

That night she took Billy and Chloe to her health
club as guests and they all went for a swim. A
couple of quick laps left her breathing hard enough
to consider quitting smoking for the three mil-
lionth time since she had started. She sat on the
side of the pool with Chloe while they watched
Billy perform like an Olympic contender.

"Billy told me what happened this morning,"
Chloe said, "and I'd say that was great timing."

Caroline nodded in agreement. 'I really think it
did the trick; not a word from Duffy all day."

"I hope you don't mind about—"

"Of course not. I think it's terrific."

"Duffy is sure going to be madder than hell

though. He'd never tolerate the idea of you sleeping with another man."

"I was counting on that."

"You don't think he'd do anything to Billy, do you?"

"You know him better than I do, Chloe."

"No. I don't think he would."

"Don't worry about Billy—he can handle himself."

"He sure can," Chloe said, her face blushing red.

Caroline excused herself to work out on the weights and later turned down an invitation to go to the movies with them. She figured the young lovers needed some time to themselves and she was sure she no longer needed their protection.

With the exception of preparations for her trip, the next two weeks were uneventful.

The DUFFY LOVES CAROLINE sign was replaced by the MURRAY HILL SECURITY sign and things seemed to be back to normal. A couple of times Caroline saw Duffy in the morning when she was going out to run, but he simply nodded his head as she passed.

At first the peace was a blessing and Caroline breathed a sigh of relief whenever she thought about how she had outsmarted Duffy. But after a few days of it, in a perverse sort of way she began to miss the element of surprise that had been such a part of her life for that brief period. She thought it was rather like a soldier must feel when there was no war around in which to participate.

The days all had a sameness about them and the only thing she had to look forward to was her trip. For that she was packed well in advance and spent spare moments taking books out of the library and reading up on the country. She was relieved that there would be no language problem as business in the Middle East was traditionally conducted in English and most of the Arab oil executives had attended either Oxford or Harvard. And if she was thrown into contact with ones who had attended Harvard, they would immediately have something in common.

While Caroline was reading up on Dubai, Chloe was immersing herself in football terminology, and Caroline was pleased she'd have someone to go to the game with. Billy was getting them both season tickets to all the Jets home games. She decided she wouldn't be a bit surprised if the two of them ended up married before the Super Bowl in January.

Billy often offered to introduce her to some of the other unmarried players, but for the moment Caroline was definitely off men. She missed Duffy at times—mostly at night and in bed—but did not seem ready to look for a replacement. And, if she were honest with herself, she'd have to admit that she still had very strong feelings about him. If he weren't so impossible, she'd probably be head-over-heels in love with him.

The week before her departure she caught herself

looking out of her apartment window at odd hours in the hopes of catching a glimpse of him. She found she was rather lonely. Billy and Chloe were always together, and while she was always made to feel welcome by them, she didn't like to intrude while they were still getting to know each other. She was often tempted to call Pat and make a lunch date, but since she was Duffy's friend more than hers she put it off. The night before she was to leave for the Middle East she phoned her parents in California.

Her father was interested in hearing about her impending trip; her mother was more interested in hearing whether Caroline had met any nice men in New York.

"One," Caroline admitted, "but he's a nut."

"A nice nut or a certifiable nut?"

"Both," said Caroline, then tried to change the subject. Her mother was relentless, though, and managed to get some information about Duffy out of Caroline. She toned it down, of course, and it ended up that her mother thought she had taken a dislike to him over his sending roses.

"What's the matter with that?" her mother demanded to know. "Your father used to send me roses."

"We're just not compatible, Mother."

"That's what you always say. You're almost thirty, Caroline, don't you think it's time you settled down?"

"Leave the girl alone," her father broke in, and Caroline silently blessed him.

Promising to send lots of postcards, Caroline finally managed to terminate the conversation and go downstairs to say good-bye to Billy and Chloe. They sat around and had a drink, toasting her success in Dubai, and then Caroline went upstairs to get a good night's sleep.

"Can I buy you a drink?" The balding businessman in the windowseat was heard from.

"No, thank you," Caroline said firmly. She opened up her briefcase and took out the papers she wanted to review before getting some sleep. She wanted to be well rested when she arrived in Abu Dhabi in the morning.

The man turned back to look out the window and Caroline sneaked a look at him. Strong features, well-dressed, really nothing wrong with him at all. No Duffy, of course, she thought to herself, then gave a vexed sigh. It was all over with Duffy, finished—there was no reason to think about him any further.

When she'd finished with the papers she put them into her briefcase, then stored it under the seat. She removed a blanket and pillow from the overhead compartment, reclined her seat, and hoped to get a few hours sleep.

"How about a nightcap?"

"I want to get some sleep," Caroline told him politely, then turned her body toward the aisle. And, unbidden, thoughts of Duffy once more invaded her thought processes. What would Duffy do in the same situation? What outrageous means would he devise to force her into having a drink with him? For one he would probably talk her to death until an alcoholic oblivion seemed preferable to listening sobriety. If he even thought that small. Never mind getting her to have a drink, he probably would have started off by hijacking the plane and forcing it to land on Staten Island.

She was just on the verge of sleep when a flight attendant came by to see if she wanted headsets for the movie. Caroline declined them, but her seat partner bought a set. Unfortunately the movie was a comedy and his laughter kept her awake throughout. She finally sat up in the seat and watched the screen, trying to read the actors' lips but failing.

When the movie was over she once again settled down for sleep, only to be interrupted by the voice beside her asking her how long she was going to be in Dubai.

"I fly back next Saturday," she told him, annoyance creeping into her voice.

"Then this will be your last drink for five days."

She thought about that for a minute, then sat up. "Okay," she said, "but just one."

She was very glad later that she actually consumed three as shortly thereafter the sun began to come up and she never would have gotten any sleep without them.

A good-looking young Arab in a Western business suit met her at the airport and she was driven to the Hilton Hotel in a limousine. The weather was very hot and very dry and she was grateful for the cool, air-conditioned interior of the Mercedes. The scenery on the drive into the city reminded her of certain parts of California, very dry, rather barren, and with an occasional palm tree standing all alone.

The Hilton was exactly like any other Hilton except that one couldn't order a drink of anything alcoholic from room service. Halim, her escort, allowed her a few minutes to drop off her luggage and freshen up, then drove her directly to the corporate offices of Mecca Oil.

Opulent was the correct word to describe the offices. She had never seen their like, even in luxurious Texas. The first thing she noticed, however, was the complete absence of women. The receptionists were male, as were all the clerical workers. She was very glad she had worn dark, conservative clothes. Even so, she felt anything but anonymous as she was ushered down lushly carpeted halls flanked with ornate gold wall sconces. Even the air seemed to be perfumed, and Caroline knew it wasn't coming from her.

The halls had been dimly lit and upon her entrance into the conference room she was at first partially blinded by the intensity of the sun coming through floor-to-ceiling windows. When her eyes finally adjusted, she saw that at least two dozen men were sitting around the immense conference table, all eyes upon her. At least they won't break into "Sweet Caroline," she thought to herself in amusement, and this thought gave her the courage to enter the room and acknowledge the introductions that were made.

She took her seat at one end of the table and the meeting began. The men were all intelligent, gracious, charming, extremely polite, knowledgeable, and fluent in English, and yet she could sense from each of them his surprise at her company's sending a woman to do the job. She was totally busineslike and used no feminine wiles, yet it was as though they had placed her on some invisible pedestal quite apart from them and nothing she was able to say or do managed, even for a moment, to put her on their level. It wasn't that the pedestal was above them: It was more as though she were on a different level entirely.

She had heard that much Arabian business, as was true of much of Europe, was conducted after business hours, usually in restaurants. She was prepared to be dined, though not wined, every night she was there, but to her surprise at the close of the business day she was driven back to her hotel in a limousine. *All right,* she reasoned, *I didn't particularly want to spend my nights discussing business anyway. This way I'll be able to see something of the city, do some shopping, maybe buy a few souvenirs.*

She took a shower in her room and changed into another of her subdued outfits, then took the elevator down to the lobby. It was literally filled with men. Men in business suits, men in flowing robes, but all men. She peeked into the hotel dining room

and again all men. Deciding she'd rather sample
the local fare than eat Hilton food anyway, she left
the hotel and started off down the street.

She was stared at, leered at, brushed up against,
and generally made to feel unwelcome, or rather
too openly welcome, and in frustration she finally
returned to her hotel. She would have dinner sent
to her room and make an early night of it.

The week passed very slowly. The days were all
right, filled as they were with business. The nights
were the loneliest she could ever remember spending. She got into the habit of purchasing the *International Herald Tribune* when she returned to the
hotel each evening, devouring every word over the
dinner she had sent up to her room. She would
then go over the business covered that day and
make notes on it, followed by writing a few postcards to friends and family in the States. By that
time it would only be around eight o'clock and
there would be nothing else to do except read the
few books she was able to find at the lobby news-
stand that were printed in English. There was no
television, no radio, and no one to talk to.

By the third night she found she was talking to
herself. Out loud. On the fourth night she began
having imaginary conversations with Duffy. She
tried to imbue Duffy with all the qualities he didn't
have, making him into a perfect dinner conversa-
tionalist, but somehow this turned out to be unsuc-
cessful. The way Duffy would actually reply to a
question kept surfacing from her subconscious,

and she found that she was actually managing to annoy herself with these make-believe conversations. And yet she liked that very annoyance. Spending her days with the overly polite Arab men was whetting her appetite for Duffy's charming candor. It surprised her to find that in retrospect it really did seem charming.

Her last night there she spent some time considering what it would be like to be posted to Dubai or one of the other Arabian countries they did business with. It had always sounded vastly romantic to her before. While she knew in reality these countries had modern cities, she had always pictured them as vast expanses of desert with an occasional Bedouin leading his camels in the distance. She hadn't pictured a society where foreign women were considered outcasts as well as untouchables. There would probably be an English-speaking colony, but this would consist mostly of married couples where she would also be something of an outcast. She decided that while she wouldn't refuse such a posting, she would certainly not seek one. And this would be as good as refusing one as most of the men she worked with desired a stint overseas. It would include extra pay and housing, but she didn't feel this would compensate for the deadly state of solitude she was now in.

This thinking naturally led to thoughts of Duffy. With no transfer overseas in the future, there was no reason for the two of them not to get together. She found she missed him dreadfully, even his more undesirable behavior. At the moment she'd even welcome a singing chicken, and she never thought she would say that. She'd not only welcome the chicken, she'd force him to sit down and talk to her. It wasn't just the trip, either. She had known every time she saw Billy and Chloe together that she wished it were the four of them, all of them having fun. She wanted to be able to run with Duffy, to be able to argue with him over dinner, to spend weekends at his house and get to know his friends. She wanted to be able to take trips with Duffy, to do even the mundane things like grocery shopping with him. And she very much wanted to be able to go to bed with Duffy at night, and maybe sometimes during the day.

In short, even when she had been raging at him the loudest, she had also been falling in love. The fact that he had been holding out for marriage at the time of their last encounter didn't bother her unduly. She had never before pictured herself as married, but then she had never before met anyone quite like Duffy. And wouldn't her mother be happy when she heard the news!

The thought occurred to her that maybe Duffy had gotten over her by now or had even found someone else. If he had really loved her, though, as he had professed, she didn't think that would be possible. She hoped it wouldn't be possible. She was suddenly longing to pick up the phone and place a long-distance call to New York to see what Duffy's reaction would be. She had the phone in her hand before she decided she could wait one more day. It wasn't something she wanted to tell him over the telephone anyway; she'd rather wait and go straight to his shop to see him when she got home.

And if he said, "Forget it, you're too late"? Then *she'd* be the one to do something outrageously romantic like filling his shop with balloons or bombarding *him* with roses or... well, she was sure Chloe would come up with some ideas.

Feeling happier than she had felt in months, Caroline packed her suitcase and laid out her clothes for her departure in the morning. She was eager to get to sleep so that Saturday would come even faster.

The flight home seemed interminable, as did the taxi ride in from the airport. What would happen if he wasn't at the shop, would she have to wait until Monday? No, she was sure Chloe would have his telephone number and address on Staten Island. She would go home first, change into something a little more colorful, and then set out to find Duffy. She had envisioned countless scenarios of their reunion while on the plane, all with happy endings, of course, and any one of them would do.

As the taxi came to a stop in front of her building, she quickly got out and looked across the street. The shop was open. Perfect!

Not even bothering to check her mailbox first, she took the elevator up to her floor and had her keys out before she even got to her door. She was so nervous it took her two tries to open it, and then she was inside and looking around the apartment with incredulity. It was absolutely bare. Charlie's smiling face was no longer on the wall, nor was her map, and there was not a single item of furniture. There was nothing, in fact, but carpeting and empty walls. She ran quickly to the bedroom where one quick look told her she had been cleaned out. The closet doors were open and not a single article of clothing remained.

Was it possible she had entered the wrong apartment? This slim hope was dashed when she retraced her steps and checked the number on the door. Against all the odds, her burglar-proof apartment seemed to have been cleaned out by a professional. She couldn't even call the police—even her telephone was gone.

In shock, she headed downstairs to inform Chloe.

Chapter Twelve

Chloe opened the door to her frantic knocking, and looking into the interior of the apartment Caroline could see Billy's familiar form at the kitchen table, one of the cats draped over his lap.

"Hey, welcome back—you really look beat."

"I've been robbed," Caroline tried to say, but the words didn't come out on the first attempt. She took a deep breath to steady herself, then repeated what she had said.

"Robbed? You haven't been robbed. Come on in; Billy and I were just having a beer."

"Great to see you back, Carrie," said Billy, opening the refrigerator and handing Caroline a beer.

Caroline set the unopened beer can on the table. "Chloe, listen to me. He's come back again and this time he took everything."

"Who came back?" asked Billy.

"My apartment was broken into about a month ago, but that time he didn't take anything." She headed for the phone on the kitchen wall. "I'm going to have to use your phone to call the police, Chloe—he even took that."

"Don't, Caroline," said Chloe. "You weren't robbed."

Caroline gave her friend an impatient look. "If you don't believe me, just take a look upstairs."

"I already have. I helped him."

"You helped someone rob Carrie?" asked Billy, looking totally confused.

"Not rob—he was just moving her stuff out."

"And you *helped* him?"

"I think you better explain," said Caroline, sinking into one of the chairs and opening the can of beer. She had a faint idea even then of what was coming.

"Let me get this straight," said Chloe. "You didn't give Duffy your permission?"

"I haven't spoken to him in weeks."

"You didn't talk to him on the phone when you were in Dubai?"

"I just said I haven't spoken to him."

"Ohmigod," said Chloe, collapsing into her chair. "I really believed him. I will kill that con man when I see him again."

"You better tell us about it, honey," said Billy, looking at Chloe with concern.

"It was last night. He came by and said that you two were getting married, that you'd called him from Dubai and everything had been settled. He said you were moving in with him as soon as you got back and would get married as soon as possible."

"And you believed that?" asked Caroline, despite the fact that it had very nearly happened the night before.

Chloe rubbed her eyes with her hands. "He seemed so happy, Caroline—so thrilled that it was happening. And I guess I wouldn't have thought even Duffy would have that much nerve."

"You gotta hand it to the guy," said Billy, a look of awe on his face.

Caroline felt as though she had been stabbed in the back. She had come home ready to forgive Duffy, ready to admit her love for him and even marry him if that was the only way to get him. And before that could even happen, he had had the unmitigated gall to take it upon himself to steal all her belongings and involve her unsuspecting friend in the deceit. This was the worst he had done yet, and she'd never, never forgive him for it. She had had a momentary lapse in Dubai, due mostly to her isolation there, but now circumstances were forcing her to quickly come to her senses. She hated him now as much as she had thought she loved him the night before. And, once again, he had placed her in the untenable position of looking very foolish indeed if she went to the police.

"Why didn't you tell me about this?" Billy was asking Chloe.

"Because you just got here a few minutes ago."

Caroline slid down in her chair and closed her

eyes. "I don't understand it. When I left town he wasn't even speaking to me, why would he suddenly start up again for no reason?"

There was a silence and she opened her eyes to see Chloe and Billy exchanging meaningful glances.

"I'm afraid that was our fault," Chloe said at last.

"How was it your fault?"

Once again Chloe and Billy exchanged glances. "The morning after you left Duffy saw me and Billy coming out of the building together. I guess he put two and two together..."

"Don't worry about it, he was bound to find out some time," said Caroline. She thought of the empty apartment upstairs. "I tell you, the way I feel at the moment I'd rather lose everything than have to see his face again. Is there some hotel around here I could check into for a few days while I decide what to do?"

Chloe's expression brightened. "I know the perfect place. The Martha Washington's just a few block from here and they only allow women. Even if Duffy found out where you were staying he'd never be able to get in. Men only get as far as the lobby."

A vision of Duffy disguised as a woman crossed Caroline's mind, but she quickly dismissed it. There would be no way for Duffy to find out where she was. "That sounds fine," she told Chloe. "Do you want to walk me over there?"

"Let's wait until Duffy closes shop for the day,"

suggested Chloe, and Caroline nodded in agreement.

A short time later there was a knock at Chloe's door. Chloe put her finger to her lips, then tiptoed over to the door and looked through the peephole. She turned to the others and nodded in satisfaction. "It's him," she mouthed, and they all waited in silence while a second knock came and then Chloe motioned that he was leaving.

Caroline went over to the front window and looked through the slats of the venetian blinds. The sight of Duffy in T-shirt and tight jeans brought an unexpected pang and if Billy and Chloe hadn't been there she would have been tempted to run after him and try to solve their differences. As she watched him get into his van and pull away from the curb, the pang turned to the more desirable feeling of cold fury and she wondered what he would do if she were to cross the street and remove everything from his shop as he had done with her apartment. She knew what he would do, though, and unlike her, Duffy seemed not to care whether he made a fool of himself. He would call the police, have her arrested, and then blackmail her with an offer of dropping the charges if she married him. She thought she was beginning to know his thought processes every bit as well as her own.

She turned back to the others. "He's gone, could we get going now?"

The Hotel Martha Washington was able to give

her a room, but one without a bath. She would have to use the community bathroom down the hall. While Billy was forced to wait in the lobby, Caroline and Chloe went up the elevator and down the hall to the room. The whole setup reminded Caroline of dormitory living.

The room was small and rather dark, but comfortably furnished, and she set her suitcase down and sat on the edge of the bed.

"This is depressing," was Chloe's opinion of the room.

"It's fine; it's just a place to sleep."

"Come on—let's get out of here. Why don't you change your clothes and we can take Billy up to see Central Park."

"All I have to change into is something very similar to this," Caroline said with a rueful smile. "Anyway, I think I'll go to the gym for a while. I haven't exercised in a week."

"How about tonight? You want to go to the movies with us?"

A dejected Caroline shook her head. "I think I'll just stay home and get drunk."

Chloe sat down on the bed next to her and put her arm around her friend's shoulders. "Come on, Caroline, you shouldn't be alone. The three of us will go out tonight and make up a new game plan."

"No, honest, I'd rather stay home tonight. I'm not used to the time difference yet and I'll probably fall asleep about seven o'clock."

"Are you sure Caroline? Tomorrow's the season

opener and Billy has to be in by eleven o'clock any-way."

"I'm sure," Caroline replied.

"Don't forget that Billy got us tickets for the game tomorrow."

"I wouldn't miss that," Caroline assured her, and after promising to call her later, Chloe left to rescue Billy from the lobby.

It was a letdown to be sitting all alone in a small room in a women's hotel instead of participating in the joyous reunion she had envisioned with Duffy. It took a great effort just to get off the bed and unpack her suitcase, thankful at least that she had cosmetics and toilet articles with her she wouldn't have to go running around to replace.

She left the hotel to go to her gym by a circu-itous route, and after working out for an hour she stopped by Wings on Third Avenue and bought herself some jeans, a sweatshirt, and some cheap running shoes so she'd have something comfort-able to wear to the game the next day. She also picked up some food at McDonald's to take back to the room with her. When she got back to the hotel she changed into her new, more comfortable clothes, devoured her hamburger and fries, then wondered what to do with herself for the rest of the evening. On a visit to the bathroom she saw lots of young women getting ready to go out that night and she began to feel as lonely as she had felt in Dubai.

It was Saturday night and all over the city

couples would be going out together, as she and Duffy could have done if he hadn't acted like such an idiot. If only he had been more patient, another twenty-four hours and they would have been together. But his lack of patience had always been the problem. Not content to let things progress naturally, he had always taken the initiative and usually with disastrous results. Did he really think the way to win her was by locking her up or kidnapping her or removing all her furniture? But then how would he know this latest method of his wouldn't bring the desired result when his first two had obviously succeeded?

She got into her cotton pajamas and propped the bed pillows against the headboard. She wished she had thought of buying something to read; there was nothing to do but sit and brood about Duffy. She wondered if her own stubbornness was as much a problem as Duffy's aggressiveness. Was he right? Did she insist on being the one to call the shots? She had, after all, been quite prepared to go back with him on her return from Dubai. The only difference now was that he had taken matters into his own hands before her arrival. *He* had been the one to call the shots. She could pick up the phone right now and call him and he'd drive in from Staten Island and pick her up and they'd spend the rest of the weekend together and everything would be wonderful.

Except that she couldn't; her pride would never allow it. She refused to be coerced into anything, and that's what it would amount to. She hadn't gotten where she was in business by making the wrong decisions and she'd be damned if she'd do it in her personal life. Furthermore, Duffy badly needed to be taught a lesson, if only she could think of what that lesson should be.

Sunday was fine with the football game and then dinner with Billy and some of his teammates. Sunday night she prepared her notes on Dubai to deliver to the department on Monday morning. She was sure that once she got back to work she'd be able to stop thinking about Duffy. She'd have to start being more sociable at work, get to know some of the men there. Duffy wasn't the only man in the world, even though he seemed to think he was.

"Congratulations," said the receptionist as Caroline got to the office on Monday morning. *On what?* wondered Caroline. *My safe return from the Middle East?*

"You're a sly one," murmured Joyce as she brought her her morning coffee. She even winked at Caroline as she left the office. Caroline gazed after her for a moment, wondering what could have precipitated the remark.

When one of the men in her group stuck his head in her office and congratulated her, a big smile on his face, Caroline began to get some inkling of what was afoot. She must have made vice-president and the news had gotten around the office. She supposed it would be announced at the meeting and she was glad she was wearing one of the businesslike suits she had bought for her trip. Not that she had had any choice in the matter, which reminded her she should spend her lunch hour doing a little shopping. Chloe and Billy had volunteered to confront Duffy that day and demand her possessions back, but Caroline had declined the offer. She would just as soon let Duffy suppose she was still out of town while she decided whether she wanted to take any legal action against him.

A phone call kept her late and she was one of the last to arrive at the ten o'clock meeting. There were a lot of smiles in her direction when she took her seat at the table, but no more congratulations. She guessed that would come after the meeting.

She gave the men a rundown on her trip, answering questions and expanding on several points when asked. The trip was considered a success, even though she related her difficulty in dealing with the Arabian businessmen at times, but that seemed to have been expected and several of the men had also run into difficulties on similar trips. She thought she had gotten the message across that she wouldn't be seeking a posting there.

Just before the close of the meeting Caroline's boss smiled in her direction and said that he heard congratulations were in order.

She didn't know what to make of his statement as a promotion wouldn't have been phrased quite that way. Her boss wouldn't have heard it, he would have decided it. He was obviously waiting for her to speak, so she finally said, "Are you referring to the trip?"

There was general laughter around the table, and then one of the men said, "It was so sudden, we've been taking bets on whether it's the chicken or one of those rich Arabs."

Caroline tried to smile but couldn't quite manage it. She looked around at the men's faces for some kind of clue to what they were talking about, but all she saw were interested smiles. "I'm sorry," she said, "maybe it's jet lag, but I'm just not following you."

"We're talking about the announcement in the *Times* yesterday," her boss told her, leaving Caroline more confused than ever.

"What announcement in the *Times*?" Even as she asked there was a sinking sensation in her stomach and she was suddenly prepared for the worst.

The man beside her cleared his throat. "Uh, what Herb is referring to, I believe, is the announcement of your impending marriage."

She had thought nothing could be worse than the chicken, but she had been wrong. This was worse than the worst; this was inconceivable. She was being made to look an utter fool and she decided the best course would be to make a joke of it.

"I don't know where the *Times* got their information," she said lightly, "but I have no plans to marry either a chicken or an Arab. In fact, to my mother's regret, I have no plans to marry at all.''

With that the meeting broke up, but her boss stopped her before she left to apologize.

"I didn't see the announcement myself," he told her. "It seems your secretary saw it and told my secretary and, well, if it really was in the *Times*, I guess you better ask them for a retraction."

Caroline laughed. "Unless my mother's seen it, it won't really matter."

Her laughter had faded by the time she got to Joyce's desk. "Just what is this about a marriage announcement?" she demanded to know.

Joyce reached into her drawer wordlessly and handed Caroline a clipping from the newspaper. Her worst fears were well-founded: There, in black and white, was an announcement of her marriage to Duffy in two weeks hence. "No calls for a while, Joyce," she said, going into her office and closing the door.

Her first thought was to call Chloe, but there was nothing Chloe could do but commiserate with her. What she really needed was legal advice. She looked in her wallet and found Pat's card, then dialed the number.

Pat was in the office and her secretary put her through.

"Pat? This is Caroline Hart, you met me—"

"Caroline! I've been hoping you'd call," Pat interrupted her. "I can't tell you how pleased John and I are that you're going to be our neighbor.

Listen, are you calling about the reception? Duffy said we'd have to get your okay on it."

"Pat, I'm not going to—"

"It's not an imposition, believe me. We'd love to have the reception for you at our place. Duffy said the wedding's going to be outdoors—"

"Pat? Please, just hold on for a moment. There's not going to be a wedding. There was _never_ going to be a wedding."

"I know how you feel. John and I did it at City Hall to avoid the fuss, but I've always been sorry."

"I'm not marrying Duffy, Pat."

"Oh, dear, you mean it's been called off?"

"It was never on."

"Then why did you move all your things out there? We spent all day yesterday helping Duffy unload the truck."

"It's a long story—"

"Sorry, Caroline, but I've got a long-distance call I have to take. Can you call me back?"

Caroline terminated the call gladly. She realized that she couldn't ask Duffy's friend for advice on how to take legal action against him. She sat there, wondering if she dared ask the company's legal department for advice, when Joyce buzzed her.

"I know you don't want any calls, Caroline, but it's your mother from California."

Caroline told her to put the call through. Her mother rarely called her at work and she again prepared herself for the worst.

"Darling, we're so happy for you. Your young

man called us yesterday and we had such a lovely talk. I feel like I know him already."

"Mother, listen to me—"

"And it was so thoughtful of him to invite us to stay at his house until the wedding. Dad and I have always wanted to see New York. Have you picked out your wedding dress yet?"

"Mother, there's not going to be a wedding."

"It doesn't have to be anything elaborate, but something in white, don't you think?"

"I'm not getting married, Mother."

There was a silence on the phone, then, "Did I hear you correctly, dear?"

"I'm not marrying Duffy."

"Oh, I know; I felt the same way before my own wedding. It's normal, darling, but you'll get over it."

In a million years I'll get over it, thought Caroline. "Mother, he is the most—"

"Yes, he's a sweetie, isn't he? He told us how he had fallen in love with you the first time he saw you, and promised your father he'd take very good care of you. And owning his own business and house? That's a good man, dear, you're lucky you found him."

It just was not possible to have a rational conversation with her mother, Caroline decided. "Look, Mother, I'm rather busy now—I'll give you a call later, okay?"

As soon as she hung up she was buzzed by Joyce. "There's a travel agent on the phone for you."

"Find out what it's about," Caroline told her.

"I already did—it's regarding your honeymoon cruise."

"Tell him or her to forget it, and don't put through any calls from now on unless they're business related. Not even my mother!"

"Uh, one other thing, Caroline..."

"What is it?"

"There's a box here from Tiffany's. It just came by messenger."

"Send it back."

"Don't you even what to see what it is?"

"In this case, diamonds are *not* forever," Caroline informed her, then broke the connection.

Caroline swiveled her chair around and looked out the window at the view from the twenty-second floor. How could one man cause her to lose complete control of her life? Could it conceivably be written in the stars as Chloe had once believed? She hadn't believed it then, but then she wouldn't have believed someone as capable as herself could have gotten into such a predicament, either. She contemplated jumping out the window as a means of solving all her problems. Then she contemplated shoving Duffy out of the window instead. The latter idea appealed to her more. She stood up, and with a decisive set to her shoulders, headed out of the office.

She gave the cabbie the address of Duffy's shop, then sat back in the seat to ready herself for the confrontation. There just had to be some way to get Duffy to listen to reason. There had to be, because she just couldn't take any more of it.

The taxi dropped her off in front of the shop and Caroline marched inside. A clerk was in the front of the store and she told him she wanted to speak to Duffy.

"The boss has taken the month off, miss—he's getting married."

The decisive set to her shoulders shifted to one of dejection as she left the shop and crossed the street to see Chloe.

"You've been getting packages here all morning," Chloe said to her as soon as the door was opened. "You must have been doing a lot of shopping."

"They're probably wedding presents," Caroline told her, moving into the kitchen and sitting down.

"Listen, do you want some lunch? I was just fixing myself a sandwich if you want one. Did you say wedding presents?"

Caroline took the newspaper clipping out of her purse and handed it to Chloe. "No sandwich, but I wouldn't mind a drink."

"That man never gives up, does he?"

"Not only that, he called my parents, and my mother, needless to say, highly approves. I also received a box from Tiffany's this morning. And he's not in his shop—I was told he took off the month to get married."

"He can't force you to marry him."

"I wouldn't bet on it," said Caroline, gratefully reaching for the drink Chloe had fixed her.

Lunch forgotten, Chloe sank down in the seat beside her. "What are you going to do?"

"I don't know, Chloe—I'm at the end of my tether."

"It would probably just be easier to marry him."

"Chloe!"

"Well, it's not as though you don't love him, and it's no good denying it to me. So he has been a little presumptuous—".

"A *little*?"

"Most women would love it."

"He just can't get away with this."

Chloe's eyes took on a gleam. "Listen, Caroline, do you want revenge?"

"Dearly."

"Then why don't you marry him, and then in a couple of months you could divorce him and sue him for all he has?"

"There's got to be a better solution."

"Do you want me to have Billy talk to him?"

Caroline gave a strangled laugh. "He'd end up convincing Billy to be best man."

Chloe nodded in agreement. "I don't know what to tell you, Caroline."

"I know." She stood up. "I have to get back to work. I don't know—maybe some solution will come to me."

When she returned to the office Joyce was chatting with a Dr. Thorgood who was waiting to see her.

"How are you feeling?" was the first thing the

doctor asked, and Caroline wondered if her boss was worried about her health and had asked the doctor to stop by.

Dr. Thorgood was opening his bag and removing a syringe, the sight of which began to unnerve her. Surely she had handled herself adequately at the meeting; they weren't planning sedation, were they?

As though sensing her fears, the doctor assured her it was just a blood test and wouldn't hurt a bit.

"Is this for my medical insurance?" she asked as the needle plunged into her arm.

"No, nothing to do with that. New York State law requires a blood test for anyone getting married."

It was too late to stop him then and Caroline could only watch with distress as her blood flowed into the syringe. Duffy again, and why was she always so unsuspecting? Probably because she expected rational behavior from people and he always came up with the irrational in any given situation.

Caroline didn't want to argue with the doctor. He had her blood, but that didn't mean she had to get married. She didn't even flinch when he left her with the promise, "See you at the wedding."

That evening after work Caroline stopped off at Saks and went straight to the lingerie department. With no bathroom to wash out her things at night she was going to have to buy some extra underwear. Passing by a mannequin clothed in a lacy white nightgown and peignoir, Caroline found herself stopping in front of it and imagining what she would look like wearing it. She didn't know why; she couldn't even imagine wearing anything but cotton pajamas to bed. And yet it was so very pretty, so soft and silky looking that it seemed almost to breath life into the mannequin.

She turned away and then looked back once again. No, it was certainly not what she needed to sleep in at the Martha Washington. In fact she would feel quite foolish wearing it to the communal bathroom. She walked over to the counter, quickly picked out several sets of panties and bras, then left the store and walked home.

Tuesday was uneventful except for the return of the package, again by messenger, from Tiffany's. She had Joyce call the store and they informed her that the ring was not returnable. To satisfy Joyce's curiosity, she opened the box to let her have a look at it. It was exquisite and obviously far too expensive, and after Joyce went into raptures over it, Caroline put it safely away, out of sight, out of mind, in her desk drawer.

On Wednesday Chloe called to say the packages were piling up in her apartment and what did she want done with them.

"Put them in my empty apartment," Caroline told her. "Duffy can come steal those too."

"Don't you even want to open them and see what's in them?"

"No," Caroline told her shortly.

The days were taking on a sameness. She worked and tried to keep her mind on what she was doing, but more and more it was wandering and she found herself making so many errors in calculation that she had to go over everything two or three times. Nights were worse. She didn't go out, not even to a movie. She had some idea she should be able to live with herself alone in a room, and even though she picked up some reading material she still found she was bored to distraction. She turned down invitations by Chloe and Billy to at least eat dinner with them, and avoided making any friendships among the women in the hotel.

Duffy managed to invade her thought processes every minute of the day; at night he dominated her dreams, leaving her tossing and turning in an effort to escape him. She loved him, she hated him, she missed him and she never wanted to see him again. Her varying feelings were at war among themselves and the more time she spent dwelling on it, the further she seemed from a solution.

On Thursday a telegram arrived at the office from her mother informing her that they would arrive Friday night and that Duffy was picking them up at the airport. From Duffy she heard not a word and she sometimes got the feeling she was existing in some sort of twilight zone where what was happening around her had no basis in reality. Everything seemed to be building up to the coming weekend and she didn't seem able to handle the simplest thing in the interim.

On Friday after work she once more visited
Saks, taking the escalator straight up to the seventh
floor. She got off, walked directly to the bridal department and pointed out a simple, elegant dress to
the saleslady.

"Do you have that in an eight?" she asked.

"Certainly."

"I'll take it," said Caroline, handing the woman
her charge plate.

"Don't you want to try it on first, miss?"

Caroline gave her a rueful look. "No. With my
luck it will be a perfect fit."

Epilogue

Sunlight streamed in through the stained-glass windows causing prisms of light to dance haphazardly on the walls and floors of the church. There was a hushed silence and then the organ began to play and the bride, a vision in white, began her slow descent down the aisle. The groom watched, a look of barely suppressed joy on his face, pride in his eyes.

Caroline felt Duffy's hand close over hers and she turned to him and said in a whisper, "They look so happy, don't they?"

Duffy didn't quite manage to stifle a chuckle. "Unlike you, my love, who looked like you were planning your escape at any moment."

"I was."

He squeezed her hand. "I never would have let you escape."

"I'm glad," she said in a soft voice, but he heard her and smiled.

"So you finally admit it, do you?"

She put her finger on her lips, cautioning him to

silence as the organ music ended. She couldn't help comparing the two weddings in her mind, and hers, she had to admit, lacked the calm dignity of the one she was now watching unfold. But how dignified can one be when instead of an organ playing "The Bridal March" a chicken is singing "Sweet Caroline"? "I'm keeping my own name," Caroline had muttered before the "I do," and Duffy, imperturbable as always, hadn't even deigned to reply.

And now, six months later, Chloe and Billy were showing them how a well-planned wedding could proceed. In spite of the singing chicken, the fall into the pool in her wedding gown and the fact that the honeymoon had to be put off since she didn't have any vacation time coming, Caroline wouldn't have exchanged her wedding for the most perfectly planned one in the world. Her wedding, with all its calamities, perfectly mirrored the bizarre courtship that had preceded it. It had been full of "Duffy-isms," and she had enjoyed every minute of it.

Billy and Chloe's reception was being held at the home of Chloe's parents on Long Island and Caroline and Duffy drove there in the BMW he had bought her as a wedding gift. She had arrived at her own wedding in a taxi.

"Were you surprised when I showed up?" she asked him now, but he wasn't in the least confused by the question.

"Not at all. I knew your innate stubbornness would have to give in at some point."

"It wasn't stubbornness."

"Call it foolishness then."

"Call it tenacity."

He laughed, a deep rumble that seemed to shake the front seat of the car, then reached over and put his hand on her knee.

"Duffy!"

In answer, his hand began to slowly move up beneath her skirt.

"You're going to cause an accident!"

"Then pull over to the side of the road."

"If I do, it will be to let you out so you can walk the rest of the way. And cool off!"

"I love it when you get mad," he said, but he removed his hand and settled back in the seat. "Are you ever sorry you married me?" he asked, his tone teasing.

"On occasion." She came to the turnoff for Smithtown and left the highway. Only a few more minutes now and they should be there.

"Aren't you going to ask me if I'm ever sorry?"

"No."

"Pretty sure of yourself, aren't you?"

"You wouldn't dare be sorry after all you put me through."

He laughed in enjoyment. "You loved every minute of it, admit it."

"That's your memory, not mine."

"All right," he conceded, "so maybe it wasn't conventional, but it worked, right?"

Caroline concentrated on the road.

"Am I right?"

She passed the right address, a large house set back from the street on what must be at least an acre of property, then kept driving until she found a parking space a couple of blocks further on. She pulled in and cut the engine. Before she could open the door, Duffy pulled her over toward him, clasping his hands behind her neck.

"Tell me I'm right."

"You're always right, Duffy."

He pulled her closer and began to kiss her. She thought fleetingly of the people passing by, then of having to redo her makeup before going into the reception. Then she stopped thinking entirely and began to devote all her attention to returning Duffy's kisses. The physical attraction between them was stronger than ever, not dimmed in any way by the familiarity of marriage.

He pulled away from her for a moment and said, "Now say it like you mean it."

"Yes, you were right; you really were."

"Damn right," muttered Duffy, then once more closed his mouth over hers. When he broke away for a second time it was to say, "Do we really have to go to that reception?"

Caroline, remembering where they were, sat back in her seat and tilted the rearview mirror down to see what damage had been done.

"I want to go—she's my best friend." She applied fresh lipstick and ran a comb through her hair, then handed Duffy a tissue to remove the traces of lipstick from his mouth.

"It's incredible," he said. "I want you as much now as I did that first time. Maybe even more."

"Me too," she admitted softly. "But I'm afraid you're just going to have to wait until we get home."

"I don't know about that."

"Duffy, don't you dare embarrass me at the reception!"

"Would I do a thing like that?" All innocence.

"Yes, you're incorrigible." She got out of the car and hand in hand they walked back to the house.

At least a hundred people seemed to be milling around the elegant living room. Caroline found Chloe and gave her a hug, whispering, "I wish you all the happiness in the world—both of you."

Chloe grinned. "If we're as happy as you and Duffy I'll be satisfied. Do you know we're thinking of buying a place on Staten Island? Billy doesn't like city living. Says he gets enough of it on the road."

Caroline thought that Chloe living near her would be the icing on the cake.

Billy came up to them and when Caroline offered him her congratulations, he said, "I hear congratulations are in order for you too."

Caroline nodded happily. She had just been made vice-president in charge of acquisitions and mergers, and while the position would necessitate traveling, relocation was not in the offing.

Someone else came up to congratulate the newlyweds, and Caroline headed for a table holding a spread of food that would have fed an army. She was filling a plate when Duffy came up to her holding two glasses of champagne. They found a place to sit down and eat and afterward followed their ears to where a live group was playing and dancing was going on.

Duffy took her in his arms and held her close, their bodies swaying to the music. There had been dancing at her own wedding, but not with live music. Duffy had brought his stereo out by the pool and the tennis courts had been used for a dance floor. They had led off the dancing and it had been the first time in weeks she had been in his arms. He had kissed her while they danced and the familiar excitement had quickly spread through her body, making her wonder why she had ever thought she wouldn't end up marrying him. Two people couldn't feel the way they felt about each other and not end up together.

Caroline's parents had flown in from California for her wedding, placing more confidence in what they had been hearing from Duffy via the telephone than what they had not been hearing from her. Duffy told Caroline's mother that if Caroline looked like her in twenty-five years he could hardly wait, and her mother had adored him on the spot. Her father had also approved, but Caroline had caught him looking at the singing chicken with some trepidation. She thought of explaining to him why the chicken was there but finally decided he would never understand. She didn't think her father had ever been a crazy romantic like Duffy.

His parents had seemed every bit as pleased about the wedding as her own, his mother confiding to her that she had been afraid Duffy would never find the right girl and his father telling her he never thought Duffy would get so lucky.

Her thoughts came back to the present when she heard Duffy whisper in her ear, "Can we leave yet?"

"Not before the bride and groom, Duffy."

"Why not?"

"It's just not done." Although "not being done" had never stopped Duffy before.

"Do you think they'll be as happy as we are?"

"No one could possibly be as happy as we are," Caroline told him.

"Umm, you're right," he murmured looking down at her, his eyes mirroring the love in hers.

And she was.

ANNE MATHER

The world-renowned author of more than 90 great romances,
including the runaway bestseller *Stormspell*,
continues her triumph with...

WILD CONCERTO

Her second blockbuster romance!
Big exciting trade-size paperback!

A bizarre twist of fate thrusts the innocent Lani into
the arms of a man she must never love. He is Jake
Pendragon, a brilliant concert pianist romantically
involved with a beautiful international opera star—
who just happens to be Lani's mother!

**A searing story of love
and heartbreak,
passion and revenge.**